THE GUARDIAN'S LEGACY

CELTIC CURSES
BOOK TWO

L.M. HATCHELL

The Guardian's Legacy

Celtic Curses (Book 2)

First published by ALX Publishing 2023

Cover Design by Atra Luna Book Cover Designs

Editing by Cissell Ink
& Two Birds Author Services

Copyright © 2023 by L.M. Hatchell

All rights reserved. No part of this publication may be reproduced, stored or transmitted in any form or by any means, electronic, mechanical, photocopying, recording, scanning, or otherwise without written permission from the publisher. It is illegal to copy this book, post it to a website, or distribute it by any other means without permission.

This novel is entirely a work of fiction. The names, characters and incidents portrayed in it are the work of the author's imagination. Any resemblance to actual persons, living or dead, events or localities is entirely coincidental.

For my early readers, for your tough love, words of encouragement, and never-ending patience with my terrible understanding of commas

CHAPTER ONE

Four weeks. That was how long had passed since I'd fucked up and released magic back into Ireland. So I'd been told, at least. I'd yet to see a single rainstorm of toads, blood moon, or hell, even a rabbit pop out of a hat to prove that was true.

As I closed the deposition I'd been typing up for my boss, I couldn't help but wonder what it would be like if that magic was real. I wouldn't be stuck here looking at the same boring legal stuff day in day out, that was for sure.

"Aisling, good, you're still here. I need you to do something for me."

I froze, a fraction of a second away from shutting down my computer when my boss's nasally voice smashed any hopes I had of escaping at a reasonable time. Overcome with the urge to bang my head against the desk, I clamped my lips shut against the groan that threatened to escape and turned to face Clifford Mercer.

Smith & Mercer is a highly prestigious law firm. You're lucky to work for them. This is just one more step towards the promotion you've been promised. I repeated the mantra silently to myself and waited with a carefully schooled expression to see what fun task was in store for me on this fine Thursday evening.

Tall and reedy with pinched features, my boss bore a remarkable resemblance to a weasel. The comparison was only heightened further by his personality, but as he was one of the founding partners of the firm, I made a point of keeping that opinion to myself.

Clifford thrust a thin manila envelope at me. "I need you to entertain a client. Mr. Athanosios is coming in to collect this, and I need you to take him out to dinner. This deal is very important, so see to it that he's looked after."

"This evening?" I croaked, failing to keep the incredulity from my voice despite my best efforts.

I was used to my boss taking liberties, but this was really taking the piss. It was five o'clock for god's sake, and he was telling me now? For all he knew, I already had plans for the evening. I didn't, but that wasn't the point.

"When else?" he asked, clearly oblivious to my irritation.

Not waiting for me to respond, he snatched his briefcase up from the floor and strode for the door. "Make sure to turn off the lights when you're leaving," he called over his shoulder. "The energy bills are criminal these days."

With that parting instruction, he disappeared, no doubt on his way to the six-figure diesel-guzzling car he kept in a private parking space below the office block – a space that likely cost more than my annual salary to rent given our offices were in the heart of Dublin city centre.

I gaped at the now empty doorway, wondering what the hell had just happened. How had I gotten stuck with entertainment duty? Surely if the client was so important, Clifford should bloody well be the one to take him to dinner.

Not for the first time, I thought about walking out and never looking back.

I'd strongly considered it after the whole magic fiasco last month – resigning, starting fresh somewhere new.

Not that Smith & Mercer had any part to play in my screw-up, really. But the firm represented the Order of the Fomori, a modern-day society that stemmed from the ancient race of the Fomorians. And the Order most definitely had played a part. A very big one.

Descending from the Tuatha Dé Danann, my family line had apparently been assigned the role of Guardian to Ireland's magic. The Tuatha sacrificed most of their own race to stop their sworn enemies, the Fomorians, from claiming it, and I, being the current Guardian, was meant to ensure that sacrifice hadn't been made in vain.

Of course, nobody bothered to bloody tell me any of that. So, when a trip to an old graveyard resulted in a seizure and some not so fun nightly visions, the Order took advantage of my ignorance by sending in Bres, their most charming representative.

He convinced me that the Tuatha Dé Danann were evil, that they were trying to use me to regain access to our world so they could enslave us all. He failed to mention that he was a lying sack of shit, and the ritual he wanted me to conduct to stop them would actually release the magic I was meant to safeguard.

Since I'd discovered the truth – too late – on the summer solstice, anything that made me think of Bres or the Order only served as an uncomfortable reminder of my naivety. Smith & Mercer fell into that category, and the sickening twist of shame that followed me into the office every day had almost been enough to make me quit.

Unfortunately, pride was one thing; money was another. And I didn't have the luxury of ignoring the latter.

So, I sat staring at the glowing screen of my computer as it mocked me for once again being a doormat. Well, screw this. I might have to give up my evening to babysit one of our pompous, rich clients, but I wasn't going to make myself useful while I waited.

For the second time, I moved to switch my computer off. A polite clearing of the throat stopped me in my tracks, and I yelped in surprise.

"Apologies. I didn't mean to startle you."

I jerked my head up to find a man with tanned skin and eyes as dark as his finely tailored charcoal suit watching me from the doorway. He was cleanly shaven and not a strand of his black hair dared to move out of place. A hint of amusement tugged at the corner of his lips, reducing the weight of his imposing presence only marginally.

Flustered, I pushed back from my desk and stood, offering my hand in greeting. "Mr. Athanosios?"

The man inclined his head and strode into the office to shake it. His grip was neither limp – the worst kind of handshake – nor did he try to demonstrate the size of his dick by crushing the bones of my hand. He went up marginally in my esteem for this, but as I was still irritated at Clifford's decision to effectively pimp me out, I refused to let myself be impressed.

During my time with the firm, I'd met many of our V.I.P. clients. The man before me didn't look familiar, and I was vaguely curious as to what could be important enough for him to traipse across the city to collect an envelope himself. A courier could've easily been arranged – and I wouldn't have been expected to wine and dine *them*.

I pushed the thought away before it could show on my face and held the envelope out to him. There was nothing on the outside to give away the contents, just a single word stamped in bold text: *Confidential.*

"I believe this is for you."

He didn't even glance at it as he took it, instead

seeming to assess me. "Please, call me Dothur. I do apologise for inconveniencing your evening..."

"Aisling," I supplied.

"Aisling." He rolled my name on his tongue, his smooth accent making it sound impossibly exotic. "Well, Aisling, I've been informed that you are my chaperone for the evening?"

I pasted what I hoped was a professional smile on my face and reached for my bag. It really wasn't the client's fault that my boss was a dick; there was no point taking my irritation out on him.

Dothur watched me with a contemplative gaze as I – finally – switched off my computer.

"While I would be honoured to have the company of a lovely lady such as yourself for dinner, I can't help but feel it's unfair of your firm to place this requirement on you," he observed.

"We're always happy to accommodate our clients." *Ugh, I think I just puked in my mouth a little.*

A quirked eyebrow and flash of amusement in his dark eyes told me he didn't buy my bullshit any more than I did. "Be that as it may, if you have other plans for the evening, I would be happy to free you from this obligation. Your boss need not know."

I eyed him suspiciously. Nothing about his expression suggested he was being anything other than genuine in his offer, but it seemed a little too good to be true. Was he really giving me the chance to gracefully bow out and avoid an awkward evening of small talk?

He waited patiently while I waged my internal

debate, and I grudgingly allocated him some extra brownie points for not being pushy.

Teagan, my best friend, lectured on ancient civilisations to her adult night class on Thursdays. Since she'd kindly donated her spare room until I got back on my feet after a breakup, I'd be going home to an empty apartment to heat up leftover curry for one. Not exactly a wild night.

Or ... I could go to dinner with him.

Admittedly, he was quite handsome, and while the dinner would be purely business, it never hurt to have a nice view while I was doing my duty as the obedient paralegal. Besides, Clifford would no doubt grill me tomorrow, and even if Dothur kept quiet about me bailing, my boss would sniff out the lie in a matter of minutes.

Before I could rethink, I found myself saying, "We can't have a valued client eating alone, now can we?"

More than one pair of female eyes followed Dothur with interest as a waiter led us to a table at the back of the small restaurant. The looks I got as his companion of choice were less friendly.

The Millstone had a charming rustic décor, and the soft glow of candlelight gave the place a more romantic atmosphere than I'd envisaged when agreeing to dinner. Still, I'd heard good things about the restaurant, and I couldn't deny that my companion for the evening looked pretty tasty, too.

I gave the waiter a polite smile as he pulled out my chair and set menus in front of us.

"We'll have the smoked salmon to start. The fillet steak, medium rare," Dothur said, as soon as the man had finished reeling off the specials. "And a bottle of Châteauneuf-du-Pape."

He handed the menus back before I'd even had a chance to open mine, and the waiter scurried off, carefully avoiding my surprised gaze.

I raised an eyebrow. "Bit presumptuous. How do you know I like any of those things?"

Dothur gave me a devilish wink, unperturbed. "Because you're a lady of good taste."

I crossed my arms and fought to keep my expression unimpressed despite the smile that set my lips twitching. "I could have a fatal allergy to fish for all you know."

"Do you?"

"No, but I could."

"I'd be happy to administer CPR if you need it."

I froze, my breath stalling at the comment.

It hadn't been so long ago that Bres had playfully offered me his CPR services. He'd been handsome and charming too, and I'd let it cloud my judgement. Maybe this had been a mistake. Maybe I shouldn't be here.

Dothur frowned, clearly noticing my reaction. "If

you're concerned about an allergic reaction, we can order something else."

What? Oh.

I snapped out of my morose thoughts, annoyed with myself. What was I doing? Dothur wasn't Bres. He'd been nothing but polite and charming, and here I was freaking out about a perfectly innocent comment. *Dammit, Aisling, at least try to leave your crazy at the door for one night.*

With what I hoped was a reassuring smile, I shook my head and laughed. "Sorry. No, what you ordered is fine." I smoothed the pristine white tablecloth out in front of me, squirming self-consciously under the weight of his dark gaze.

Thankfully, the waiter chose that moment to return with our bottle of wine, shifting the attention from me. He presented the bottle to Dothur for approval. "Would Sir care to sample it first?"

Dothur waved away the offer, and the waiter proceeded to pour the wine. I watched the ruby liquid slosh into my glass and silently hoped that I could make it through the dinner without spilling it on the beautiful tablecloth.

"So, where are you from, Dothur?" I asked once the waiter was finished and had scurried away again. "That's definitely not an Irish accent."

His lips quirked up at my genius observation. "Indeed. I'm from Greece. My brothers and I are here for a few weeks on business."

"Oh, really? Can I ask what kind of business?"

"It's a family business. We deal in natural energies."

I took a sip of my wine and winced a little at the vinegary taste. Would he be insulted if I ordered a different drink?

"Interesting," I said, pushing the glass away – I'd stick to water. "Did your brothers come to Ireland with you?"

"Yes. Ireland has a special place in my family's history, so when the opportunity arose to return, we couldn't turn it down."

"Oh, you've been here before?"

"A long time ago. Tell me about yourself, Aisling."

His dark eyes met mine, and I felt my cheeks heat as he focused the full weight of his attention on me.

"Not much to tell." I shrugged a little self-consciously. "I'm a Dublin girl, born and bred. I've worked for Smith & Mercer for three years, though I always secretly wanted to join the circus. But shh, don't tell anyone," I told him with a conspiratorial whisper.

He laughed at that, a rich, sensuous sound that sent a shiver of delight through me.

I had to give it to the man, he was the personification of sexy. Tall, dark, and handsome, wrapped up in a well-dressed package, and finished off with a yummy accent. I could almost forgive Clifford for dumping this dinner on me last minute. Almost.

The waiter returned then with our starters in hand, and for a few minutes we ate in companionable silence. I caught Dothur watching my reaction more than once, but I stoically refused to let him see just how much I was enjoying his choice. Admittedly, though, it was some of the nicest smoked salmon I'd ever tasted.

"What about your family? Are they from here also?" Dothur asked before taking a sip of his wine – I couldn't help but notice that he didn't wince at the taste.

"Yep, one hundred per cent Irish." I dabbed my mouth with my cloth napkin and pushed away my empty plate. "My mam was born in Wicklow and has never left since. She and my dad separated when I was a baby, so I don't remember much about him, but I believe he was from Dublin."

"No siblings?"

"Nope, only child. Teagan, my best friend, is the closest thing I have to a sister, though I always wanted a brother when I was younger. Are you and your brothers close?"

He tilted his head, considering the question. "Sometimes it feels like we've spent many lifetimes together. It makes for both an unbreakable bond and a regular desire to, how do you say, throttle each other."

I snorted out a very unladylike laugh at his choice of phrase, the sensual accent making it sound completely out of place. "Sounds like an interesting dynamic."

He gave a wry smile. "Family. Can't live with them, can't live without them."

CHAPTER TWO

A gentle breeze ruffled my hair, and I raised my face to the warm sun that shone overhead. Somewhere in the distance, birds chirped and the trees whispered their secrets to each other. The meadow I sat in was surrounded by rolling hills as far as the eye could see, and the grass beneath me was so soft that if I closed my eyes I could almost imagine I was floating on a cloud.

None of this should have been possible, of course. The heat of the sun shouldn't have rejuvenated me the way it did. I shouldn't have been able to run my fingers through the rich, green grass, and nature's fragrant aroma shouldn't have drifted to me on the breeze. Because this was all a dream.

Almost every night for the four weeks that had passed since the solstice, I'd found myself here in this place. It had become almost as real to me as the waking world, though logically I knew that was crazy. Still, the calm of my surroundings lulled me into a state of relaxation, my mind drifting to memories of my dinner with Dothur.

As it turned out, the evening had been very enjoyable. Dothur had managed to find quite an appealing balance between being intriguing and cultured, while also showing genuine interest in my more mundane life. He'd apparently enjoyed our time together too, as we parted with him asking for my phone number. I knew it wasn't wise to get involved with a client of the firm, but he was only in town for a few weeks. What was the harm in a bit of fun?

"You're not concentrating."

I cracked an eye open to find Killian slouched against a nearby tree with his arms crossed, an expression of bemused exasperation on his face.

My dream mentor ran a hand through his light brown jaw-length hair, clearly trying to rein in his frustration at his wayward student. As always, he wore faded jeans and a black shirt with the sleeves rolled up. I'd asked him once where he got the clothes from, since fashion had changed drastically from the time the Tuatha Dé Danann – and therefore, he – had last roamed our world. He'd cryptically said something about appearing to me in whatever form made it most likely for my mind to accept his presence. The idea had hurt my head and raised even more questions than it answered, which was not helpful in the slightest.

"It's hard to concentrate with you staring at me," I pointed out, though in truth I'd been so lost in my thoughts that I hadn't even realised he'd arrived. "What's the lesson for today, boss?"

"Meditation."

I groaned. We'd been at this meditation crap for weeks now, and I still sucked at it. Seriously, how was it possible to empty your mind and think of nothing? The very fact of telling yourself to stop thinking produced a thought in itself; it made no sense to me.

Still, Killian was the magic expert, so as always, I humoured him and closed my eyes.

"Clear your mind," he instructed, and instantly thoughts multiplied in my head like horny bunny rabbits having an orgy. "Listen to the world around you. Feel it. Let its energy wash over you, fill you."

I focused on the low, soothing cadence of his voice, and slowly the thoughts faded away.

"You are the Guardian," he continued. "Your very being connects you to the magic. You just have to open yourself to it."

Open myself. Sure, I can do that. I'm an open door.

As I had many, many times before, I waited. What I was waiting for, I didn't really know. A bolt of lightning? A glowing light bulb to appear over my head? A sudden shifting of my world view that would make me wonder how I'd been so blind up to this point?

But just like every other time, nothing happened.

With a huff of frustration, I flung myself back on the grass and opened my eyes. "Do we have to keep doing this? It's been a month. Surely we'd know by now if the magic was back?"

There was a long silence before I sensed Killian move to my side. He sat down next to me, draped his arms over his bent knees, and stared out into the distance.

"The magic is back. I wouldn't be here with you now if it wasn't. But things are very different in your world now."

My world. I didn't miss the phrasing, or the careful way he kept his tone neutral as he said it.

It had once been his world too. A very long time ago.

Just as my role of Guardian had been built into the sacrificial ritual conducted by the Tuatha Dé Danann, so too had Killian's. He was a fail-safe of sorts. It was the Guardian's job to protect the gateway to the magic. Killian's was to deal with the fallout should the Guardian fail.

He'd told me this when he'd first come to me in my dreams. Actually, his exact words to me had been, "You've really fucked it now," but then he'd at least proceeded to fill in some of the many gaps in my knowledge.

What he hadn't told me was why he'd volunteered for the role. Considering it had resulted in him being held in stasis for millennia before finally being awoken thanks to my naivety, I couldn't help but be curious about his motives.

"What do you mean things are different?" I asked.

"The technological advancements that have been made are nothing short of magical in themselves, but they are man-made. The destruction of nature for the sake of progression has changed things, and it will impact the speed and form in which magic returns. The only question is how."

"If all these advancements are such a big block, how can you be sure it will return at all? Maybe the ritual did work, but the magic just isn't strong enough to overcome the changes?"

The corner of his lip twitched with amusement he was clearly trying to contain, and I scowled at him.

"The magic is tied to the land. The land will always be stronger, no matter how much the ignorance of man damages it."

I thought of the natural disasters that were occurring more and more frequently around the world, and I found I couldn't quite disagree with his point. Even in Ireland the signs of global warming were becoming visible on a daily basis, and I'd often wondered how much of it was nature fighting back against our so-called progress.

When I didn't argue, Killian gave me a considering look. He extended his hand and slowly rotated it from side to side. Sparks of green light crackled and skittered along his skin. It appeared almost like electricity, but he didn't flinch at its touch, so I had to assume it wasn't hurting him.

"The magic is in its purest form here," he said, staring at the light. "Frozen at the point in time just before the Tuatha sacrificed themselves to protect it." He snapped his hand closed and the sparks winked out. "But if you don't believe, it might as well not exist at all."

Silence settled between us as I considered his words. He made it sound so simple; just believe, and *poof!* Magic. That was all well and good, but what if I never got the hang of it? Sure, I was the Guardian, but I'd already proved I sucked at that, so who was to say I wouldn't suck at this magic craic too?

I pushed myself back up to sitting and huffed out a breath. "Is it really so bad if I can't use it? I mean, let's say the magic has returned and I never manage to access it. Does it really make a difference?"

"When magic was last part of your world, the Fomorians stopped at nothing to control it. Do you think the Order of the Fomori will be any different? Times may have moved on, and their methods may have changed, but I can guarantee you they haven't. They've used you once to get what they wanted. They'll do it again."

My throat burned at the reminder of how I'd allowed myself to be manipulated.

When Bres first approached me, I'd been convinced he was a conman. No matter how sexy and charming as he was, talk of ancient races and magical visions would be enough to send any woman running a mile. But then the visions – or dreams, as I'd thought them to be – started taking their toll on me. I'd have done anything to make them stop.

Since the Watchers of Danu, what remained now of the Tuatha lineage, hadn't bothered to clue me in on my heritage, I'd thought I was going nuts. And when Bres offered me not just proof of his tale, but also a solution to save my sanity, I'd left all reason at the door and followed him blindly to the conclusion he'd been steering me towards all along.

The visions had stopped as soon as I completed the ritual; that much he'd been honest about, at least. Instead, they'd been replaced by nightly magic lessons with Killian in this dreamscape. It was safe to say I was a pretty crap student, though maybe if I got a cool wand or something I'd feel motivated to try harder.

As it was, I brushed off his comment with barely concealed vehemence. "I won't be stupid enough to fall for their lies again."

Shadows darkened his brown eyes and he turned his gaze away from me. "There are many ways to mislead with the truth, too."

I searched his expression but found it as unreadable as ever. I sighed.

"They haven't come near me since the solstice. They got what they wanted. Surely I'm of less use to them if I stay magically impotent."

In fact, nobody had come near me since the solstice – not the Order, and not the Watchers of Danu. The former was a welcome relief, the latter downright pissed me off.

The Watchers had known all along that I was the Guardian and had left me to flounder in my ignorance until it was too late. They'd claimed not to want to burden me with the responsibility unless it was absolutely necessary. What was their excuse now?

Killian pushed himself up from the ground and offered me his hand with a crooked smile that didn't quite chase the shadows from his eyes. "Humour me."

Huffing to ensure my martyrdom was clear, I accepted it and stood.

"Close your eyes," he ordered, and I did.

The heat of his touch caused my skin to tingle, and the rhythmic flow of his words lulled me back into that relaxed state. I allowed my mind to drift, considering what it might actually be like to have magic.

Killian had explained that magic came from the life force of all living things. In humans, it took different forms depending on a person's natural affinity, but in theory, we all held that energy inside us. Accessing it was a whole different ball game, however.

The thought drifted away as Killian guided me through the now-familiar meditation. My breathing relaxed and my body became heavy as my weight sank down into the earth, grounding me. Bit by bit, the tension left my body.

The gentle tug beneath my belly button was so subtle that at first I thought my imagination was playing tricks on me. It was an odd sensation, almost like a rope that connected me to something unseen.

My eyes flew open. "I think –"

As quickly as it had come, the feeling disappeared.

I pressed my hand to my abdomen, looking down in wonder. Had I imagined it?

I opened my mouth to voice the question aloud, but before I could speak, an alarm clock blared. The meadow dissolved around me, taking with it whatever tenuous thread I may or may not have discovered to the magic.

CHAPTER THREE

Spooning a second serving of lasagne onto my plate, I allowed my mind to wander from the buzz of conversation that surrounded me. I both envied the easy chatter of those seated around my mother's large oak dining table and took comfort in its familiarity.

The annual O'Meara family dinner was one of the few occasions when my mother's family all gathered together and got reacquainted away from the hustle and bustle of life. Normally I looked forward to catching up with my relatives, but after everything I'd recently learned about my family tree I couldn't help but look at them all in a new light.

My mother came from a small family by old Irish standards. By the time she and her two siblings were born, my granny had declared in no uncertain terms that she was shutting up shop for good. Given the horror stories my mam had often told me about my own birth, I couldn't say I blamed my granny.

According to Killian, the magic for the Guardian's role had come from a powerful female mage who was so far back in my lineage that I didn't even try counting how many "greats" separated us. Because her magic was the source, the role of the Guardian was passed solely through the blood-related females in my family.

As it stood, there were three generations of females from the O'Meara bloodline sitting around the table this evening, giving four potential candidates – my granny, my mam, my aunt Rachel, and me. I eyed the other women and marvelled at the ridiculousness of the situation.

The magic automatically gravitated to the strongest available candidate alive at any point in time. It wasn't a huge stretch to see how I might be a better candidate than my ninety-year-old granny, or my mam, who was often away with the fairies even before magic had been a factor. My aunt, however, was intelligent and responsible, the serious one in the family. She'd never have been stupid enough to get tricked into releasing the magic. So, why had I been chosen over her?

Granny O'Meara jabbed her fork in my direction from where she sat hunched in her chair at the head of the table, interrupting my internal debate. "Where's that handsome young man that normally accompanies you to dinner, Aisling? What was his name again? Paul? Patrick?"

A deafening silence fell over the room, and I squirmed as my relatives all carefully avoided looking at me.

My mam had given everyone a heads-up about my break-up with Pete to avoid me having to answer awkward questions such as this, but god bless my granny, her memory just wasn't what it used to be.

"I think you mean Pete, Mother," my mam clarified before I could answer. She patted my hand and gave me a smile that was no doubt meant to reassure me that she'd handle this, but only made my stomach clench in trepidation.

That prophetic feeling was given life barely a breath later when she continued, "Remember I told you he and Aisling had separated? He proposed to her and she broke up with him. That takes a lot of courage, you know."

I dropped my head to the wooden table, unable to suppress a groan. Where was a good hole when you needed one to swallow you up?

Knowing that I needed to intercede before my mam made things even worse, I pasted a smile on my face and straightened up. "It really wasn't quite that dramatic. Sometimes relationships just don't work out."

It was true, though, that I had broken up with Pete in response to his proposal. The sense of dread that had filled me when he uttered the words "Will you marry me?" was a hard sign to ignore, and I cared too much about him not to be honest. Walking away from everything we'd built over three years together had been hard, but he deserved better.

"You a lesbian?" Uncle Jack asked, his words half

muffled thanks to the enormous fork full of food he'd just shovelled into his mouth.

His wife, Betty, glowered and clipped him across the ear. He gaped at her with a confused expression, providing a graphic view of said food in the initial stages of mastication.

"What? I never said there was anything wrong with it, did I? Just, she's shacked up with that girl now, hasn't she? It's a fair question."

I looked between the two of them, a little lost for words at the turn the conversation had taken.

As my mam hurried to remind them all that Teagan and I had been best friends since childhood and it stood to reason that I'd want to stay with her while I got back on my feet, I once more wondered what idiot thought my family would be the best choice for such a hefty responsibility.

Observing the conversation with an amused expression, my cousin Jennifer leaned across the table and stage-whispered to me, "If you don't have a thing going with Teagan, feel free to pass on my number. She's hot."

I bit my cheek to hold back my chuckle. With her sleek black hair and flawless pale complexion, my best friend was often mistaken for Megan Fox. It wasn't unusual for a near-equal ratio of men and women to hit on her when we were on a night out, so my cousin was far from being in the minority with her observations.

"Aunt Betty," I jumped in, more than ready to

redirect the attention away from me and my life. "How's your gout?"

Just like that, the conversation shifted back to the mundane family updates that I'd been counting on to distract me this evening. I nodded sympathetically as my aunt bemoaned the pains of growing old. Rolled my eyes as my mam regaled us all with the horror story of her recent internet dating attempt – her second one in as many months despite claiming the first had put her off men for life. And had to suppress a yawn as Uncle Jack's update on his recent stock investments caused more than one pair of eyes to glaze over. It was so normal, and I loved every minute of it.

When everyone had had their fill of food, I jumped to my feet and began cleaning up, grateful to have a few minutes to myself. The lively chatter followed me into the kitchen and I wrapped it around me like a comfort blanket.

This was what I needed. More normality, less crazy theories about magic and ancient feuds. It didn't matter who my ancestors were; these people here now were my family. So, as I stacked the dishwasher, I made a conscious decision to put all thoughts of the past to the back of my mind for the evening.

Feeling lighter than I had in a while, I topped up my glass of wine and went to rejoin the others. I walked out of the kitchen just in time to hear Granny O'Meara adamantly declare to the room, "I'm telling you, the fairies are back."

I closed the door of Teagan's apartment behind me and leaned back against it, letting my eyes close for a moment. Situated close to Dublin city centre, the open plan living space was cosy and welcoming, and best of all, it was blissfully empty. The tension slipped from my shoulders, but still the niggle of unease stayed with me.

My family had been quick to dismiss my granny's strange comments as old age ramblings, but her words had shaken me, and I'd made an excuse to leave early.

Did fairies even exist? I had no bloody idea. But given how strange the last few weeks of my life had been, I was afraid to discount anything lest I tempt faith.

Teagan would be home from her evening classes shortly, and I contemplated opening a bottle of wine while I waited for her to return. Though she hadn't been caught up in this whole mess herself, she'd acted as a voice of reason for me ever since I'd confided in her. Her love of ancient civilisations and all things mythology meant she'd been equal parts intrigued and sceptical when I'd filled her in on everything that had happened. She never doubted that I was telling the truth, however, and for that I was eternally grateful. She helped keep me grounded, and I badly needed that right now.

Though drowning out my thoughts with wine was appealing, I opted instead for some brain-dead entertainment. I snuggled down on the puffy grey sofa and switched on the television to reveal a sombre news reporter on the screen. Her tone was suitably grim as bold, attention-grabbing headlines scrolled across the bottom of the screen: *gruesome murders leave community in shock as second body found.* I quickly flicked over to the next channel – I had enough problems without adding nightmares to the list.

Settling on a home renovation program, I soon found myself imagining how I might decorate my house – if I ever managed to afford one. Given I was now ticking the "single" box on the mortgage application forms, I was likely to be nearing retirement by the time that happened. Still, I indulged myself, and was so caught up in the daydream that I almost jumped out of my skin when my phone buzzed on the sofa beside me.

Dothur's name flashed up on the screen, and a smile ghosted on my lips as I opened the message.

I enjoyed our dinner. Meet me on Sunday. 3pm.

Wait, was he asking or telling me? I scowled at the screen. What a presumptuous git! Still, I couldn't help my smile from breaking through.

Mixing work with pleasure wasn't the best idea, but he was only in town for a few weeks while his business deal was being settled. I couldn't deny that I'd enjoyed our dinner the night before, and it wasn't often a handsome, charming man asked me out. Maybe it was time I had a bit more fun?

My internal debate didn't last too long, and I was just hitting send on my reply when a key jangled in the lock of the front door. The greeting I was about to issue froze on my tongue as Teagan appeared in the doorway. Her eyes were red and puffy, and it was clear she'd been crying.

I jumped up, hurrying to her side. "What happened? Are you okay?"

She clutched her coat tighter around herself as if to stop her visible shaking, and the watery smile she gave me did little to ease my growing concern.

"I'm fine," she said with a sniffle.

I eyed her sceptically, scanning for any obvious signs of injury that could explain her clear distress.

Teagan dropped her bag by the door and looked around, her expression bewildered. "I don't know what's wrong with me. One minute I was teaching and everything was fine, the next –" she shook her head. "I just felt this overwhelming sense of sadness. I can't explain it."

"Did anything happen in class?"

She shook her head again.

"Hormones?" I suggested gently. Though for the life of me I couldn't remember a time I'd ever seen Teagan succumb to something as mundane as PMS.

For mere mortals like me, it was pretty standard to require a tub of ice cream at regular monthly intervals. Teagan, however, seemed to navigate the minefield of menstruation like she did everything else in her life –

with grace and an unshakeable confidence. Now, she just looked lost.

"Maybe," she said, as much to herself as in acknowledgement of my question. "I think I'll just have a bath and go to bed."

I gave her shoulders a quick squeeze before nudging her towards the kitchen. "Why don't you let me run the bath for you while you make yourself something to eat? I know I always get emotional when my sugar levels are low."

She didn't crack so much as a smile at that, despite being well aware of how poorly I functioned when hangry. Concerned, I watched her trudge to the fridge, open the door, and stare blankly inside. I hoped she wasn't coming down with something.

CHAPTER FOUR

eagan's muffled voice came to me through the haze of sleep I was trying to groggily extricate myself from. I blinked, wincing at the sunlight that streamed through my bedroom window, and wondered how the hell it was morning already. The sound came again from the living area, not clear enough for me to make out what she was saying. But her voice registered sufficiently through my brain fog for me to realise something was off with her tone.

Curious, I shoved the covers off before I was tempted to return to blissful oblivion. I slipped my feet into the fluffy unicorn slippers that waited next to the bed, pushed away the last vestiges of sleep, and shuffled out of the room.

I found my friend sitting on the plush grey sofa, a strained rigidity to the set of her shoulders. Her phone was pressed to her ear, and her knuckles were blanched white due to the death grip she held on it.

The tears glistening in her eyes jerked me to a stop. She looked up at me with a mask of shock on her face and hung up the phone without saying goodbye.

"What's wrong?" I hurried to her side, pulling her into a tight embrace. My mind offered up a platter of worst-case scenarios for what might have happened, but I pushed them firmly away.

For a few never-ending moments, Teagan just clung to me in silence. When she finally spoke, her voice was dull, emotionless.

"One of my students was killed on her way home from the lecture last night." A sob broke free and she covered her mouth as if she could physically stop the grief from escaping. "She was murdered."

I tightened my grip on her, holding her close as I processed her words. Unwittingly, my mind flashed back to the news report I'd caught a snippet of the night before. Surely it wasn't connected. Horrible things happened all the time, even in a smaller city like Dublin.

Teagan took a shuddery breath and pulled away from me. She stared at the floor, looking completely lost.

"I didn't even know her that well. The summer school students are with me for such a short time and..." She dropped her head into her hands as another sob broke free. "Niamh came to me at the end of class yesterday asking for help with an assignment. It was right around the time I started feeling off, and I just wanted to get out of there as quickly as I could. I asked her to come back to me next week. Maybe if I'd..."

Before I could interject and reassure her that she most definitely was not to blame, Teagan pushed off the sofa and bolted for the bathroom. A moment later, the sounds of retching reached my ears.

I didn't have the strongest stomach for dealing with vomit, but there was no way I was going to leave my friend alone in that state. So, I grabbed a glass of water from the kitchen and followed her.

I found her huddled in a ball on the bathroom floor, shivering. Her normally pale skin had turned a worrying shade of grey, the lack of colour even more noticeable thanks to her red-rimmed eyes. Crouching down beside her, I brushed her hair back from her face and offered her the glass.

"Can I do anything?"

The look she gave me was so forlorn that my heart ached. "I think I'll just go back to bed."

Wrapping my arm around her, I helped her up from the floor and led her to her room, tucking the blankets in tightly once she was settled in the bed. She shivered despite the heat in the apartment, and I couldn't help my frown of concern.

"Are you sure I can't get you anything?"

Her eyes had already drifted closed when she mumbled her reply, so I left her to rest, closing the door quietly behind me after a final worried glance.

Taking into account her student's untimely death, and the guilt she was wrongly piling on herself, it was understandable that Teagan wasn't bouncing off walls with happiness. But given her strange mood the night before, and her unhealthy pallor, I once more wondered if she was coming down with something.

Maybe I should call a doctor?

Of course, given it was a Saturday my chances of getting one to even answer a phone were slim to none. Which left me the option of bringing her to an over-crowded emergency department. Since a minimum twelve-hour wait time was unlikely to do much to ease her grief, I decided to shelve that idea. Sleep would be the best thing for her right now.

A sharp rap on the front door broke through my thoughts, and I looked at it in surprise. Teagan's apartment was part of a larger complex that included gated security. Normally we had to buzz any visitors into the main entrance before they could reach our door, and I couldn't think of any reason the neighbours might be calling.

I opened the door, assuming the caller had the wrong apartment. A tall woman with ginger hair paced on the other side, clearly agitated with the whole sixty seconds it had taken me to answer.

"Siobhán," I stuttered, more than a little surprised to find her there.

A month had passed since I'd last seen the Watcher of Danu or her partner, Brian. They'd been the ones sent to approach me when the Watchers had finally decided I deserved to know about my role as Guardian. Things hadn't gone quite as expected.

As part of his master plan, Bres had set it up to make it look like Brian was trying to kidnap me so that he could then swoop in to save me and gain my trust. Naturally, I'd had a hard time believing anything the two Watchers tried to tell me after that. At least until I realised – too late – that it was Bres who was the liar.

The last encounter I had with Siobhán had resulted in her lying unconscious thanks to the shock wave I'd inadvertently caused by releasing magic. I felt bad for running away like a coward, but I'd been terrified and confused, and in my defence, I'd made sure she and Brian were uninjured first. Still, it didn't stop the shame that heated my cheeks now.

Siobhán finally stopped her pacing and raised an expectant eyebrow. "Are you going to stare at me all day, or can I come in?" She filled the doorway, making it clear that she wasn't leaving even if I said no.

I was tempted to, nonetheless. Maybe I could close the door and pretend she wasn't there?

Unfortunately, my mother raised me with manners, and years of conditioning refused to let me to be rude now. So, I grudgingly stepped aside and allowed her to pass. The apartment felt smaller with her in it, and I fidgeted awkwardly by the door.

She was wearing jeans and a sweatshirt instead of her Garda uniform, so I had to assume she was here on behalf of the Watchers rather than police business. For some reason, that made me feel more nervous rather than less.

Was she here for an apology? She was probably

owed one. But the words stuck in my throat, choked by the bitterness I couldn't help but feel towards the Watchers of Danu for leaving me to flounder.

"Have you been watching the news?"

I blinked, taken aback by the unexpected direction of the conversation. What had the news got to do with anything?

Clearly taking my blank look as a no, she continued without waiting for a response. "There have been deaths. Sacrifices. The police are keeping the exact details from the media so you probably wouldn't have made the connection, but they are – connected, that is."

My mouth went dry as my mind jumped again to the news report, and then unwittingly to Teagan's student. "How ... how are they connected?"

Siobhán's lips flattened into a grim line as her jaw clenched. "All the victims were members of the Watchers of Danu."

Her words hit me like a slap in the face. Numbly, I made my way to the kitchen table and slumped into one of the chairs. "What were their names?"

There was a flash of surprise that quickly shifted to suspicion. "Why?"

I glared.

"Fine. Amy, Keith, and Niamh."

And with that final name, all the air seemed to be sucked from the room.

I dropped my head into my hands, my thoughts in turmoil. Oh god. How would I tell Teagan? Should I even tell Teagan? She'd been so upset at finding out her student had been killed, but sacrificed? It would destroy her.

Why was Siobhán even telling me this, anyway?

If she was looking into the victims' backgrounds, surely she'd have come in an official police capacity to speak to Teagan. She hadn't though, which suggested she was here because of my connection to the Watchers.

Which was stupid. Aside from sharing an ancestral line, I had nothing to do with the group, and I was more than happy for it to stay that way. This had nothing to do with me.

When the silence became almost unbearable, I looked up to meet Siobhán's unyielding gaze. My stomach flipped at the determination I saw in her eyes.

I swallowed, my mouth dry. "Why did you say the murders were sacrifices?"

"They all had a ritualistic element. The Gardaí suspect satanic cults are involved, but I think we both know the truth."

"Do we?" I scrunched my brow, irritation at the cryptic comment momentarily overshadowing my shock. "What truth is it exactly that I'm supposed to know?"

She crossed her arms, her expression making it clear that she thought I was being obtuse. My irritation flared into outright anger and I had to force myself to take a slow breath.

"Why are you here, Siobhán? I'm sorry to hear about your friends, I honestly am. But I don't know why it has anything to do with me. I'm not part of your little club, and I sure as hell don't know anything about murders or" – I shivered and wrapped my arms around my midsection – "sacrifices."

Her expression turned hard as stone. "You're Tuatha. Whether you like it or not, you're one of us. That puts you in the firing line too."

"I'm one of you when it suits," I snapped, unable to rein in my anger any longer. I pushed back from the table and stood, throwing up my hands in frustration. "If I'm supposed to be part of this great big family, where have you all been for the last month while I've been driving myself mad, waiting for the other shoe to fall?"

She sighed. "We've been cleaning up your mess."

The note of weariness that edged her tone made me hesitate. What did that mean? What had they been cleaning up?

Panic bubbled up inside me, exacerbated by the fear and uncertainty that had been simmering in my gut for the past four weeks straight as I'd wondered what the repercussions of my actions would be. I pushed it away, instead pulling my anger to me like a comforting suit of armour.

"A mess that never would have happened if the Watchers hadn't left me to figure this Guardian shit out for myself. Bres might have been a manipulating bastard, but at least he was there."

She sneered, her features twisting in disgust. "And you fell for his charm, hook, line, and sinker."

Oh, that's it. I was done with this conversation. "It's not like anyone else was offering to help. And when things went to shit, you just disap –"

"Hey. What's all the yelling about?"

I turned in surprise to find Teagan propped against the door frame of her bedroom, a frown creasing her forehead. She looked from me to Siobhán and froze.

A strangely vacant expression settled over Teagan's face. Her eyes widened in shock as she stared at Siobhán, and for a moment I thought I saw them flash purple. Suddenly, she crumpled to the floor.

"Teagan." I ran to her side, all else forgotten in my concern for my friend.

Her skin was clammy, coated in a sheen of sweat, and I cursed myself for being so quick to dismiss the idea of bringing her to the doctor.

Carefully, I rolled her over onto her back, cradling her head in my lap. Her chest rose and fell in a steady rhythm that only marginally assuaged my panic. A quick scan showed no obvious signs of injury, but her eyes remained closed, her skin ashen.

"Bring me my phone," I called out to Siobhán. It didn't matter if it meant a painfully long wait in the emergency department. I was going to right my earlier mistake and get Teagan to a doctor.

My phone didn't appear, however, and I looked up, irritated.

The Watcher hadn't budged from the spot where she'd been prior to Teagan's appearance. Instead, she was staring at my friend's unconscious form, her own skin gone a worrying shade of pale too. Her mouth was set in a grim line of determination, but I could've sworn it was fear that shone in her green eyes.

I looked from her to Teagan with the uneasy feeling that I was missing something important. "Siobhán?"

The Watcher flicked her gaze back to me, as if only just remembering I was there.

"They'll be coming for you too," she said, the hard edge gone from her voice. "Help us stop this."

With that, she picked up my phone from where it lay on the kitchen table and brought it to me. She gave a final wide-eyed look at Teagan, then turned on her heel and left.

CHAPTER FIVE

Teagan threw me an exasperated look from the far end of the sofa where she was cocooned in a nest of blankets and cushions. "You know this isn't helping," she admonished, her tone not unkind.

She was right, but I couldn't stop myself from flicking over to yet another news station as I hugged my cooling cup of tea to my chest and scanned the headlines that flowed along the bottom of the screen.

We'd spent almost fifteen hours in the emergency department after Teagan's collapse the previous day. Given the type of casualties the weekend attracted, we'd been provided with riveting, if not disturbing, entertainment for much of the long, uncomfortable wait. My personal favourite had been the drunk guy who pissed around all the chairs in the waiting area, insisting that he was creating a protective circle so the demons wouldn't get us.

In the end, the doctors hadn't been able to find

anything wrong with Teagan, and all the tests had come back normal. They'd sent us home citing a possible virus combined with the stress of her recent grief, but I had my doubts.

Even now that the colour had returned to her cheeks and she'd regained some equilibrium following the news about her student, I couldn't help but sneak furtive glances her way to reassure myself that she was okay.

Though I'd given her the gist of Siobhán's visit, I hadn't had the heart to tell her that it was very likely her student had been one of the victims. I wasn't sure how much she knew about Niamh's death already, but somehow I didn't think mentioning that she'd been sacrificed would be helpful for Teagan's recovery.

As the thought came into my head, I realised with a flash of guilt that what I was doing now – obsessively checking the news – probably wasn't helping either. At best, it was bloody morbid. At worst, there was a chance they would mention the victim's names and my attempt to save Teagan that pain would've been for nothing.

I quickly changed the channel, stopping only when I came to one of the game shows we enjoyed. "You're right. Murder updates aren't recommended Sunday watching," I acquiesced with a forced smile.

For a while, I let myself become absorbed in our usual routine of shouting answers at the television. We groaned and shook our heads when the contestants failed to heed our clearly genius suggestions, and brushed it off when our answers were so far off the mark that we might as well have been playing a differing game entirely. But try as I might, I couldn't push all thoughts of the murders from my mind.

"Would the police really be able to keep it quiet?" I blurted out during one of the ad breaks. "I mean, if all the murders had a sacrificial theme, surely the media would've been all over that like flies on shite. There have been three deaths already."

Teagan considered that for a moment. "Maybe. But even if Siobhán was telling the truth about that, it doesn't mean she was telling the truth about the rest – about you being in danger."

I curled my knees into my chest and wrapped my arms around them, hugging them tight. Was that even the part that was bothering me? Or was it something else that I didn't want to admit?

Dublin wasn't immune to its share of serious crime. Generally though, the motives for murder were clear: rival gangs seeking payback for some slight or other, a dealer sending a message about unpaid drug debts, an abusive partner that wasn't stopped in time.

These murders were different. Despite the lack of real detail being broadcast, the news reports made it clear that they were all connected. The suggestion of a possible serial killer was enough to make anyone feel uneasy, regardless of the manner in which the murders occurred.

"Do ... Do you think it could have anything to do with what happened..." The words lodged in my throat.

I swallowed back the fear and forced myself to say it aloud. "On the solstice, I mean. With the ritual."

"Siobhán didn't say anything about magic, did she? There could be all kinds of reasons why someone is targeting the Watchers of Danu." She shrugged. "Who knows what goes on in these strange cults."

She seemed so certain of what she said, no doubt evident in her tone. I sought solace in that confidence, even though I didn't quite feel it myself.

I'd been hoping to speak to Killian about Siobhán's visit last night. I hoped maybe he'd be able to shed some light on her motives, though why I thought that, I wasn't sure. It didn't matter anyway since he was inconveniently a no-show.

A thoughtful expression settled over Teagan's face, and she turned to me, her blue eyes glittering mischievously. "What power would you wish for if you did have magic? I think I'd want something really cool, like the ability to control the elements. Or, ooh, telekinesis, so I could do all the boring housework without lifting a finger."

I sighed. "I'm perfectly happy without magic, thank you." My thoughts shifted to the odd feeling I'd had a couple of nights previous. I'd been so sure at the time that it was magic I'd felt, that I'd finally found a connection to it after all these weeks. But maybe it was just my imagination playing tricks on me, the way someone lost in the desert hallucinates about finding water?

"If my lessons with Killian have taught me

anything, it's that I am no magical prodigy," I said wryly. "The best I could probably hope for is to be able to float a pen someday."

"Never underestimate the damage you can do with a floating pen."

I snorted out a laugh.

My phone buzzed on the chair beside me, and I looked down at it in surprise. Dothur's name showed up on the screen and I cursed. I'd forgotten all about dinner.

I waged a mental debate with myself. Between Siobhán's visit and Teagan being unwell, my head was up my arse; I'd be terrible company. Maybe I should just cancel?

Teagan stretched out her foot and kicked me. "Don't even think about it," she warned, clearly reading my mind. "You are going on that date. It'll do you good to get out of the house and take your mind off things."

A protest lay on the tip of my tongue, but I hesitated. Sitting around all morning had done little for my mood, and I couldn't imagine a few more hours would improve it. Still, I was reluctant to leave Teagan alone, given her collapse the day before.

"Go," she insisted again. "I'm fine. The doctor said I just need to rest. I promise I'll call if I don't feel right."

I scrutinised her for any sign that she was putting on a brave face to set my mind at ease. I couldn't deny that she looked a lot more like herself today, and though I'd acted as army sergeant, refusing to let her budge from the sofa all day, she hadn't seemed to be showing any continued side effects from whatever had caused it all.

Another push from Teagan's foot sent me reluctantly to my feet. With a pointed look from her, I went to find something to wear. She was right, I needed to get out of the house and stop driving myself mad. Besides, what was the harm in having dinner with a handsome, charming man anyway?

I parked the car and checked my make-up one final time in the mirror. Once I'd brushed the metaphorical dust off my little black dress and gave myself permission to look forward to my date with Dothur, I'd instantly felt better. Sitting around overanalysing every detail of Siobhán's visit wasn't going to solve anything, and it was no doubt what she wanted me to do.

There was a nervous flutter in my stomach as I climbed out of the car. Unlike our previous dinner, this actually felt like a proper date, and I was glad I'd insisted on meeting him in town so that I had time to compose myself beforehand.

The evening had grown cool, so I grabbed my jacket and made my way towards Dawson Street. FIRE Steakhouse and Bar was situated in the Mansion House, a beautiful old Victorian building. I'd heard fantastic things about their food, and a quick peek at their menu online had set my mouth watering.

As I approached the building, I spotted Dothur

waiting outside. I was surprised to see he wasn't alone. A tall man with broad shoulders and pitch-black hair pulled into a low ponytail stood next to him. I couldn't hear what either man was saying from where I was, but it was clear from their agitated gestures that the conversation was heated.

Before I could get close enough to ascertain what was going on, the second man threw his hands up in the air and stormed off in the opposite direction from where I was approaching.

I watched him leave as I drew up alongside Dothur, suddenly a little wary. "Everything okay?"

The smile he gave me was every bit as charming as I remembered. Any tension he held from the previous interaction seemed to just disappear as he leaned down to kiss my cheek.

"Family," he said, as if that explained everything. "You look ravishing."

I returned his smile and pushed my lingering curiosity aside – he was only here for a few weeks and this was just a bit of fun; his family dramas were his own problem. With that in mind, I took the arm he offered and allowed him to lead me into the restaurant.

CHAPTER SIX

Killian had barely reached the log where I was perched before I blurted out, "Siobhán came to see me yesterday."

Despite the welcome distraction of my date with Dothur, Siobhán's visit hadn't been far from my mind. By the time I got home I'd been restless and eager to speak to Killian. Only Teagan's insistence that I share every detail of my evening had delayed me in making a beeline for my bed.

Thankfully, I hadn't had to wait long before I found myself in the familiar meadow. Killian had been slower to appear, however, and the skin around my nails was now significantly worse for wear thanks to me picking at it while I'd waited impatiently.

"The Watcher?"

I nodded. "There've been murders. Sacrifices, or so I'm told. All the victims were members of the Watchers of Danu."

He frowned but didn't say anything as he came to lean against the tree next to me.

"Siobhán tried to convince me that I was in danger. No doubt it's another one of the Watchers' games." The words sounded like wishful thinking even to my own ears, but I grasped at the possibility nonetheless.

"What kind of sacrifices?"

I blinked in surprise. Morbid much! "How should I know? It has nothing to do with me?"

When he didn't immediately agree with me, the thread of unease that had been winding its way around my insides tightened its grip. It wasn't unusual for Killian to act as the voice of reason when it came to anything related to the Watchers; he was technically their ancestor after all. He always allowed me the freedom to rant without judgement, but then he had this annoying habit of presenting a calm, rational argument if not in their favour, then at least to assuage my irritation.

Despite that, I'd been hoping he'd laugh off Siobhán's warning of danger. Instead, there was an undeniable tension in his shoulders as he pushed away from the tree and came to stand in front of me.

"We can't waste any more time. Let's get started."

I gaped at him in confusion. "That's it? You don't have any thoughts on the murders or what Siobhán said?"

A shadow passed behind his eyes and his mouth set into a grim line. "You need to train."

A loud banging jolted me awake and the meadow disappeared, taking Killian and his hours of drill sergeant training with it. The sudden shift from the bright sunshine of the dreamscape to the almost complete darkness of my bedroom caused my chest to tighten in a moment of panic before it registered that I was awake.

The pounding came again, more insistent this time, and I realised it hadn't been part of the dream but rather someone knocking on the front door. I leapt out of bed and hurried to answer it before the noise could wake Teagan – or the rest of the apartment block for that matter.

Pulling my dressing gown tight around me, I opened the door to find a stocky man with a shaved head standing on the other side, his hand poised to strike the door again. The rebuke I'd planned died on the tip of my tongue as I took in Brian, Siobhán's police partner and fellow Watcher.

Unlike when Siobhán visited, Brian was wearing his Garda uniform. Dark circles were apparent under his eyes and a five o'clock shadow covered his jawline, giving him a somewhat dishevelled appearance despite the pristine clothes.

My surprise shifted to anger. It was bad enough to be woken at an ungodly hour, but for a visit by yet another Watcher – one that I disliked even more than the last – was just taking the piss. I gripped the door tightly, not willing to offer even the suggestion that he was welcome. I'd learned from my mistakes.

"What do you want?" To hell with being polite; if the darkness in the apartment was any indication, this was not an acceptable time for social calls.

"Siobhán is dead."

The words hit me like an anvil and I stumbled backwards, releasing my iron grip on the door. That didn't make sense. I'd spoken to her less than forty-eight hours ago.

Brian didn't wait for an invitation to take advantage of the now unmanned door. He followed me into the apartment, closing the door behind him. When he turned to look at me, it was with an expression of utter weariness.

Thanks to Bres' machinations, Brian and I had taken an instant dislike to each other when we met. I thought he was an aggressive knob who was trying to kidnap me and force me to release the "evil" Tuatha Dé Danann. He thought I was betraying my cause by shacking up with the Order and helping them to release magic.

The fact that all of this came about because of a series of misunderstandings changed nothing. First impressions were hard to shift.

Now, though, there was nothing menacing or intim- idating about the man, and for a brief moment, sympathy overshadowed any antagonism I felt towards him. I had no idea if he and Siobhán had been friends, but they'd worked together, and it was clear he'd been knocked sideways by her death.

"Can I get you something to drink?"

The offer was a meagre truce in the face of his loss, but he nodded, accepting the olive branch for what it was.

"Tea would be good."

Neither of us spoke as I boiled the kettle and laid out mugs with milk and sugar. I waited until we were both seated at the kitchen table before quietly asking, "What happened?"

He scrubbed a hand over his face. "Siobhán said she came to see you? She told you about the sacrifices?"

I nodded, my hand involuntarily tightening around my mug.

"After she spoke to you, she sent me a message saying she had a lead. I was on duty, so I told her to wait for me. It wasn't safe to go alone."

"She didn't listen," I guessed.

He grimaced. "She was impatient like that. People were dying – people we knew and cared about. Neither of us liked the idea of sitting around twiddling our thumbs while more people got hurt, but it was only a few hours, dammit. That's all she needed to wait. Instead, she went and got herself sacrificed."

I hissed in a breath.

Though I knew very little of the specifics behind the actual murders, my brain helpfully conjured up horrific images and plastered Siobhán's face on them to ensure I felt the full impact of the news. I hugged my mug of tea to me, but the warmth did nothing to thaw the icy chill that settled over me.

Brian reached into his pocket and pulled out a crumpled white envelope. He shoved it across the table towards me, glaring until I took it. My name was written in neat handwriting on the back. No address, no stamp.

"What's this?" I asked, eyeing it warily.

"Open it."

I crossed my arms and looked him square in the eyes, waiting.

He let a frustrated sigh. "Siobhán stopped by the station before she... She left this with the officer on the desk with a message for me to make sure you got it if I didn't hear from her."

"Me? Why me?"

He didn't answer, but he didn't need to. Siobhán had said it herself on Saturday – she thought I could somehow help stop the murders. What made her think that, I had no idea.

The silence hung expectantly between us so, with trembling hands, I tore open the envelope and pulled out the letter inside. Careful not to tear it, I unfolded the page.

The same neat writing that had been on the envelope flowed across the paper, and a quick glance at the signature confirmed that it was from Siobhán. Delaying as long as I could, I examined every aspect of the note until eventually I could delay no more. I started to read.

If you're reading this, then I'm dead.

I stuttered to a halt at the very first sentence, almost dropping the page. My heart pounded as I read it again, needing to be sure my imagination wasn't playing tricks on me. When it became clear that wasn't the case, I forced myself to swallow and read on.

The words that followed were simple, matter of fact. They contained none of the emotion you'd expect to accompany such a declaration, and I could almost hear the cold detachment behind them. Siobhán reiterated her belief that I was in danger, declaring in no uncertain terms that it was my *duty* to stop the sacrifices, given they were most likely connected to my recent fuck-up – her words, not mine.

The suggestion caused my insides to churn sickeningly, but what followed stopped my heart cold.

If my death isn't enough to encourage you to help, then maybe you'll do it for your friend. The magic has returned. Its impact is minimal right now, and I'm sure you've even managed to convince yourself that the whole thing was a bad dream. It wasn't. The magic is here, and your friend is already suffering because of it.

Teagan's reaction when she saw me was enough to warn me of what's coming. But it was nothing compared to how she'll be affected when the magic grows stronger. She needs to learn how to control her powers, or they will control – and destroy – her.

The Watchers of Danu can help her. Work with Brian to bring an end to this, and they've given their word that they will guide Teagan in understanding her new nature.

I stared at the words, my fingers tightening on the letter until the page crumpled in my grasp.

"What does she mean?" I demanded through clenched teeth. "What's wrong with Teagan?"

Brian's expression was blank as he met my gaze. "Help me stop this, and I'll tell you everything."

CHAPTER SEVEN

The morning sun had yet to make an appearance on the horizon as I climbed out of Brian's Volvo and followed him – reluctantly – to the black wrought iron gates of St. Stephen's Green park. I hadn't imagined when he demanded my help that it would involve me attending a crime scene, yet here I was.

My excuse about needing to get to work had fallen flat given the still ungodly hour, and Brian had reminded me with a vindictive satisfaction that if I wanted answers about Teagan, I had no choice but to play ball. So, wrapping my arms tightly around my midsection, I took in the strangely silent park before me.

Normally, St. Stephen's Green was teeming with people. The large pond beyond its entrance was home to many a hungry duck waiting for scraps of food to be flung their way, and the park itself attracted even more pigeons than it did people. Today, though, it was missing those vibrant signs of life.

Uniformed Gardaí manned the barrier that had been formed with bright yellow police tape, while other men and women kitted out in protective clothing conducted a search along the distant tree line. It was like something from TV, only this was real life, and I couldn't just change the channel.

Brian had warned me on the drive here that Siobhán's body was still at the scene and that it wouldn't be a pleasant sight. It hadn't seemed to register with him that a civilian might wind up needing a lifetime of therapy after something like this, or that bringing me here wasn't exactly appropriate. To him I was no longer a person; I was the Guardian. Which clearly meant that traumatising me for life was a more than acceptable option.

Tension hung heavily between us as he raised the police tape for me to duck under. Silently, I prayed for one of the other officers to stop us and question my presence, but no such protests were forthcoming, and I found myself one step closer to seeing my very first dead body.

A deep, primal instinct screamed at me to turn back before it was too late. I wasn't brave. I was the person who cowered behind a cushion waiting for the bad guy to jump out in the movie. It was only concern for my best friend that kept me moving forward despite my clammy palms and the growing tightness in my chest.

"All the Watchers have been issued with tracking

devices given the recent deaths," Brian explained as he led me towards a clearly marked trail in the nearby trees. "There's a panic alarm built into each one. Siobhán triggered hers at midnight. Our people got here quickly enough to find her before a civilian could stumble upon the scene, but not quick enough to..."

There was no emotion in his voice despite the muscle that ticked at the side of his jaw. I marvelled at his ability to remain detached when discussing something so horrific; I was ready to vomit with the nerves somersaulting in my stomach and we hadn't even gotten to the body yet.

Clearly fate had a grudge against me because a moment later Brian came to a halt. The subtle stiffening of his shoulders was the first indication that we'd reached the spot. The foot I glimpsed on the ground just beyond him was the second.

Bile rose up in my throat and I squeezed my eyes closed, forcing myself to take slow, deep breaths. It was fine. I could do this.

The smell of decay that I'd expected to act as an early warning was oddly absent. How long did it take for a body to start smelling anyway? I had no idea. Surely there should be a metallic tang of blood at least?

The very fact that I didn't know the answer highlighted exactly why I shouldn't be here. What could I possibly tell Brian about the murder that he couldn't figure out for himself?

If he was expecting me to be some freaky metal

detector for magic, he was going to be sorely disappointed.

Knowing I was likely signing myself up for a lifetime of nightmares, I peeled one eye open and then the other. I focused on the broad expanse of Brian's back as I tried to prepare myself for what was to come. When he stepped to the side to clear my view, I couldn't put it off any longer. I cast my eyes down.

The image didn't make sense at first. It was like someone had taken a jigsaw puzzle and mixed up all the pieces. I could make out the shape of a body, sure. But it was as if my mind had no frame of reference to decipher the rest.

Siobhán – because as much as I wished otherwise, it was her – lay spreadeagled on the ground. Her arms and legs were stretched out so that they touched the edge of the circle that had been gouged into the earth around her. It reminded me of a pentagram, though I wasn't sure if that was just what I expected a sacrifice to entail.

I couldn't take my eyes from her face. Someone had crudely carved the number four into her forehead, but despite that, her expression was peaceful. It didn't make sense.

"Her heart is missing." Brian's voice jolted me out of my thoughts, and I flinched. "Same as the other victims. There's not enough blood, but the coroner doesn't think the body has been moved. More likely she was drained."

For the first time, I truly looked at the rest of the

body. My mind rearranged the pieces of the jigsaw with the added clarity provided by his words until the picture came into high definition focus.

Siobhán's chest cavity was splayed open, pieces of gleaming white bone visible between the sinew and muscle. The incision ran from her collarbone to her pubic bone, and I noted with a numb sense of detachment that it seemed to be an extremely neat parting for something so brutally violent.

I had to swallow a number of times before I found my voice again, but try as I might, I couldn't seem to pull my eyes away from the body. "What would they want the blood for? You're not going to tell me there're such things as vampires, are you?"

"Blood is life. Whatever it's being used for, it can't be good."

With a vague sense of bubbling hysteria, I noted that he hadn't answered the second part of my question. I swallowed again, my mouth barren.

"Do you have any idea what the sacrifices are for?" I gestured helplessly to the body, beseeching him to make sense of a situation that had no justifiable explanation that I could see. "What could someone possibly hope to achieve from this?"

"You tell me," he demanded, crossing his arms as he planted his feet firmly in place.

I gaped at him, incredulous. "How the hell would I know?"

The situation was so absurd I'd laugh if I wasn't standing here staring at an actual dead body. I was so out of my depth that I was quickly being dragged out to sea, and as much I'd love to be able to Sherlock Holmes this for him, I literally had zero idea how I could contribute.

"You're not even trying." He gestured angrily to the body. "See that circle? This is a magical ritual. Magic *you* released. So you can cut the ignorance bullshit and start making yourself useful."

A bone deep chill washed over me at his words. I stared at Siobhán's lifeless body, horrified. Had I done this? Was this my fault?

My stomach lurched. Covering my mouth with my hand, I turned and fled back down the trail we'd entered by. Brian shouted after me, but I ignored him, focused only on getting as far away from Siobhán's body as possible.

Her face followed me as I ran, the image of it frozen in that oddly peaceful mask in my mind. Would I have looked so peaceful lying there in her place? Surely she'd been terrified.

Oh god.

Tears stung my eyes as I clambered under the police tape. The black gates straight ahead promised an escape from the chilling scene I'd left behind, an end to the nightmare that was playing out around me.

I was so focused on my salvation that I didn't see the man until he stepped into my path and I ploughed into his broad chest. I looked up, flustered, to find myself staring into the darkest eyes I'd ever seen.

The man wore a long black leather coat, and

despite the mild summer weather, he had the hood pulled up. Shadows danced across his face, and try as I might, I couldn't make out his features aside from the piercing eyes.

"Sorry," I mumbled. A strange mugginess clouded my mind as I met his dark gaze, and I was only dimly aware of his powerful hands gripping my shoulders.

"My fault."

His low voice sent a shiver through me, and I found myself unable to look away from the shadows that held him tantalisingly out of reach. He raised a hand as if he might brush his fingers across my cheek, and I held my breath.

"Aisling. Wait up."

Brian's yell snapped me out of my trance, and I swung around to see the Watcher striding towards me. Gasping in a shuddery breath, I turned back to find the man in the leather coat gone.

I scanned the surrounding area, my heart racing. There was no trace of him, only shadows that danced in the rays of the early morning sun. Had I imagined it all?

That moment of confusion was all it took. The gate, and my escape, grew further out of reach as Brian closed the final distance between us.

He came to a stop next to me and grabbed me by the elbow. "We need to talk."

CHAPTER EIGHT

I delved into the steaming cup of hot chocolate with my spoon, mining for the clumps of melted chocolate that had settled at the bottom. The small café was buzzing with workers queueing to get their caffeine hit after an early commute into the city centre. Few of them paused for longer than it took to order and collect their drug of choice, so it had been easy to find a somewhat private table towards the back of the seating area.

A clock ticked ominously on the wall next to where I sat, informing me that I, too, should join the scurry of the rat race if I didn't want to be late for work. I was finding it hard to care.

Across from me, Brian sipped his black coffee. The signs of exhaustion once more showed themselves in the weary slump of his shoulders and dark shadows beneath his eyes, and I had no doubt that the haunted look was mirrored on my own face.

"There was no smell. I always thought dead

bodies..." I trailed off, my brain belatedly informing my mouth just how insensitive the comment was.

The thought had been repeating in my head on loop as I tried to make sense of the scene. My mind had clearly latched onto it as the safer topic to focus on, though it said a lot about how my day was going that the smell of decomposing bodies was deemed safe. Thankfully, if Brian was bothered by my comment, he didn't show it.

"Magic works in strange ways." He shrugged. "The circle could have contained the signs of death, or maybe something about the ritual changed the natural process."

The sickening understanding that I might have had a part to play in all of this struck me once more. I pushed my cup away, the hot chocolate curdling in my stomach.

"Seems like a lot of suppositions."

He pinned me with a stony glare. "Magic has been gone for a very long time. The Watchers have preserved as much knowledge on the subject as we can, but for millennia it's been little more than theory. You're the Guardian. Do you even realise what that means? You have a closer connection to the magic than anyone else currently in existence. If anyone is able to answer these questions, it should be you."

I pushed my chair back, anger and frustration warring inside me. Did he not think I'd help if I could? "What exactly is it you expect me to do?"

"You're the Guardian," he repeated. "It was your job to

keep the magic safe. You didn't do that." He held up a hand to halt my retort. "*We* didn't do that. And now people are dying. Siobhán believed you had an important role to play, and I trust her judgement. Even if I don't like it."

A muscle ticked in his jaw, and I could almost feel the frustration oozing off him. He didn't want to be working with me any more than I wanted to work with him, but I could tell by the determined set of his shoulders that he wasn't backing down.

With an exhausted sigh, I looked up at the clock. Shit, I really was late for work now.

I grabbed my bag, relieved to have an excuse to escape this conversation and get some much-needed headspace. The buzzing of my phone on the table stopped me.

Panic tightened my chest as the residual adrenaline from the morning sent all kinds of worst-case scenarios flying through my head. It took me a moment before I registered the name on the screen: *Margaret*.

I frowned. Margaret was my ex-boyfriend's mother, and though I'd always gotten on well with her while Pete and I were together, I hadn't had any contact with her since the split.

Feeling Brian's watchful gaze on me, I answered the phone. "Margaret. Hi."

"Oh, Aisling, I'm so sorry to bother you, dear. I don't even know why I'm calling if I'm honest. I just didn't know who else to turn to. You meant so much to my Pete, and I know things are different between you now, but if anyone can get through to him then surely it must be you."

My frown intensified at her babbling. I'd never known Pete's mother to be anything other than cool and collected. She sounded genuinely distressed, however, and I couldn't for the life of me imagine what Pete could have done to upset her so much; he was the quintessential mammy's boy.

"It's okay, Margaret. Just take a deep breath. Why don't you tell me what's wrong?"

"Well, you see, that's the thing. I really don't know. He just hasn't been himself at all. He's been so angry, lashing out at everyone around him."

She was right. That didn't sound like Pete. Even on the rare occasion when we fought, Pete was usually the one to defuse the situation, his calm, reasonable mannerism making it impossible to stay riled up. I couldn't discount the idea that our break-up had negatively impacted him, and therefore his mood – I'd be heartless to dismiss his feelings like that. But the last time I'd seen him, he'd been on a double date, so I didn't think that was the reason.

Still, I had to ask, "How long has this been going on?"

"A few weeks. It was just small things at first. His sister was having trouble at work. Nothing major, but he made a big scene about her being treated unfairly. He confronted her boss, almost got her fired and himself arrested. Things started getting worse after that, but when I tried to talk to him about it, he just shut me out."

She let out a soft sob, and I crumpled inside. I could deal with anything other than the thought of the poor woman crying.

"I'm not too sure what I can do to help." I closed my eyes against the guilt that bore down on me as I uttered the words. "I haven't seen Pete in weeks. I'm probably the last person he'd speak to."

"Nonsense. Peter has no hard feelings towards you. Maybe if you just went to see him? He won't even answer the phone to me, let alone the door."

I strongly considered banging my head repeatedly against the wall. How did I get myself into these situations?

"Look, I have to get to work now, but I'll stop by his place this evening. I'm not making any promises," I hastened to add. "He probably won't talk to me."

Her profuse gratitude was ringing in my ears as I hung up the phone to find Brian still watching me with a curious glint in his eyes.

"Problem?"

"I need to go," I said, ignoring his question. "You got what you wanted. I came to the crime scene with you. Now tell me what's wrong with Teagan."

He crossed his arms in what I'd come to recognise as his stubborn bastard pose. "That's not how this works. The agreement is that you help me get to the bottom of the murders and the Watchers will help you. You're getting nothing from me before then."

It was the response I'd expected, but I still had to bite back my snotty retort. "Fine. I need to go before I'm fired."

"Call me later," he ordered, holding out a business card.

With gritted teeth, I snapped it from his grasp, then turned and stalked from the coffee shop, feeling my puppet strings pulled taut with every step I took.

<hr>

Work should have been a welcome distraction after the morning I'd had, but between Clifford's shitty mood over me being ten minutes late, the niggling concern I hadn't been able to shake since Margaret's phone call, and, oh yeah, the bloody dead body I kept seeing every time I closed my eyes, I spent the day just a tad distracted.

As soon as I could escape from the office, I hailed a taxi and headed for the house I'd once rented with Pete. I'd only returned once since our break-up, and that had been to collect my things. Now, a swarm of angry bees were wreaking havoc in my stomach at the thought of returning.

I didn't regret my decision to end the relationship. But we'd made a lot of memories in the three years we'd been together, and many of them were tied up in the house we'd shared. That was no small thing, even if I had been the one to walk away.

It was still early evening when the taxi pulled to a

stop in front of the semi-detached house in the quiet estate I'd once called home. Despite the early hour, however, the curtains were drawn across all the windows. Pete's trusty Ford sat in the driveway, but aside from that, there were no other signs of life. Maybe he'd gone away?

"Can you wait for me?" I asked the driver, who only grunted in response as I climbed out of the car.

Two wheelie bins stood next to the house, over-flowing with empty containers and rotten food. Unease settled over me.

Pete was a clean freak. He despised any kind of clutter and was a complete germaphobe; he'd never have let the rubbish build up like this.

I made my way up the driveway and rang the door-bell, shifting from foot to foot as I waited. What was I actually going to say if Pete answered? *Hey, your mammy sent me to check on you?*

My mental debate was unnecessary because the door remained firmly closed. Instead of being relieved, my concern only increased. I knocked again, pressing my ear against it to listen for any sign of movement inside.

Nothing.

I was about to give up and call it a day when I heard a soft thud.

Eyeing the door in case it suddenly opened, I crouched down and lifted the letterbox to try to peer into the hallway beyond. Thick privacy bristles blocked my view, but the smell of stale air and body odour hit me like a tangible force. I grimaced, flinching away.

"Pete," I called. "It's Aisling. I don't know if you're in there, but your mam is worried about you. I'm worried about you. Just call me, okay?"

When there was once again no response and the door didn't open, I let the letterbox drop with a resounding clunk. There was no point sticking around and talking to myself; maybe I'd come back and try again tomorrow.

Reluctantly, I made my way back to the waiting taxi. As I did, the hairs on the back of my neck prickled and I had the strangest feeling, like someone was watching me. I cast a quick glance back over my shoulder, expecting to see a curtain twitch or some other sign Pete was monitoring my retreat from inside the house, but there was nothing.

CHAPTER NINE

The sensation that someone was watching me followed me the entire way home. It didn't make sense, of course, considering how fast the taxi was moving despite the evening traffic. Still, I couldn't help my wary glance around as I finally climbed out of the car at the gates to the apartment block.

After the emotional rollercoaster of the day, every part of me was mentally and physically exhausted. I rested my head against the cool metal interior of the lift and closed my eyes for the brief moment it took to ascend to the third floor.

I was debating a scalding shower and an early night when I stepped out into the hallway and a long black box wrapped with a black satin ribbon caught my attention. It rested on the floor in front of the apart-ment door, and there was no indication from the empty hallway as to who might have left it. Curious, I hurried to see.

The box was light, and it was only when I picked it up that I noticed the small card peeking out from under the ribbon, the matte black of its surface blending with the box itself. A single word was written in an elegant silver script on the card: *Aisling*.

Surprised, I unlocked the apartment door and carried the box inside. The living area was quiet and Teagan's bedroom door stood ajar, the room beyond showing no signs of life. She didn't have any lectures on Monday evenings so my first reaction was one of worry until I spotted the note on the kitchen table.

Gone for a walk to get some fresh air. Back soon x.

I gave myself a little shake and forced myself to relax. It was understandable that I was a little jumpy considering everything that was going on, but Teagan had seemed a lot better by the time I'd returned from my date with Dothur the day before. Hovering over her like a mother hen wouldn't help anything.

Still, I couldn't shake the memory of her collapsing. Or Siobhán's ominous warning.

Mentally berating myself for letting the Watcher get under my skin, I turned my attention back to the black box. Grateful for a distraction, I untied the ribbon, letting the smooth fabric run through my fingers.

Inside the box a rose rested on a bed of black satin. The petals of the rose were a purple so dark that on first glance they almost appeared black, and a single thorn remained on the stem. I stared at it, transfixed. There was nothing inside to indicate who the sender had been, but the only possibility that came to mind was Dothur. The thought brought a small smile to my face as I closed the box back up, too exhausted to think about finding a vase right now.

I debated sending Dothur a message to thank him, but hesitated. Was that too presumptuous of me? I didn't actually know for sure that he'd been the one to send it. Maybe I'd check with Teagan first on the off chance she'd seen someone drop it off.

A quick rummage in the fridge turned up nothing that appealed to me for dinner, and since my appetite had been A.W.O.L. most of the day anyway, I opted for a shower instead.

There was still no sign of Teagan by the time I emerged, skin flushed red and wrinkled as a prune. Despite almost giving myself third-degree burns with the scalding water, a pervasive chill remained with me, and I picked out my fluffiest pyjamas in the hope of some much-needed comfort.

Brian's business card rested on my locker, and I bit my lip, debating whether or not to call him. He'd told me to, but what could I really say? *Hi, I'm just calling to highlight once again how useless I am?* I had no answers for him, and as much as I'd love to be able to say something unbelievably intelligent that would crack the case wide open, the chances of that were on par with me winning the lotto.

I couldn't face speaking to him again today, but I could think of one person who might have some answers, and that person I did want to speak to. Pulling the curtains to block out the last dregs of daylight, I snuggled up under my duvet and let the darkness take me.

Killian was already waiting when the world around me faded to be replaced by the lush green meadow. I ignored his look of impatience and jumped straight to the chase.

"I saw a dead body today."

His slight flinch was the only sign that I'd taken him by surprise. "Who?"

I dropped cross-legged onto the grass next to where he stood. "Siobhán. Turns out she got herself murdered not long after she came to see me. Sacrificed, in fact."

A pregnant silence left my words hanging in the air between us. I let it drag out as long I could before I couldn't stand it anymore.

"I think you know something you're not telling me."

He glanced away for only the briefest moment before once again meeting my challenging stare with an impassive expression. "What did the body look like?"

My jaw dropped. "Are you seriously asking me for the gory details?"

"You said she was sacrificed. There are many types of rituals that require death. The details – gory as they might be – may tell us the aim of this one."

"Oh," I muttered, only slightly mollified. I didn't want to think about Siobhán's death. I definitely didn't want to focus on the image that had been replaying itself on loop in my head all day. But if it could help end the killing, I had to try.

Swallowing past the bile that rose up in my throat, I attempted to detach myself from the memory and focus only on the cold, hard facts.

"Her torso was sliced open, her heart was removed, and her body was almost completely drained of blood. The number four was carved into her forehead and" – I had to swallow again despite my valiant effort to remain emotionless – "she looked peaceful."

Killian's brow furrowed at that, and I was glad I wasn't the only person to find that fact odd. He was quiet for a long time as he considered my words.

"There are many ritual sacrifices that require the heart and lifeblood of their victims, none of them good." He pushed a hand through his hair and stared into the distance, lost in thought. "I don't believe the number is relevant to the sacrifice itself, but it makes me think the person is treating each murder as a trophy, or working towards a particular target."

I shivered.

He blinked, snapping out of whatever thought he'd been chasing. "Anything else you can think of?"

I chewed on my lip, revising the scene in my head. "There was a circle carved into the ground around her body. And it was the weirdest thing, there was no smell or anything. Is that normal?"

"The circle would be standard practice for magic rituals. It's possible it may have delayed the natural signs of decomposition if it held the body in stasis to allow the ritual to take hold."

Magic. That's what it kept coming back to. Magic that wouldn't even exist anymore if it wasn't for me.

Killian's sympathetic look as he lowered to the ground beside me only made me more irritated, so I focused back on the facts. "What's the most likely aim of the ritual?"

"Based on what you've said? Power."

My confusion must have been clear from my clueless expression because he continued.

"Do you remember the key rule I gave you when we started our training?"

I thought back to when I'd first found myself in this place, the night of the summer solstice. Considering everything that had led up to that point, it hadn't seemed so strange to suddenly find myself with a mysterious dream tutor, though I was still pissed that the lack of magic had prevented him from coming sooner – maybe it would've saved us all a lot of trouble.

Killian had lectured me relentlessly about the responsibility that came with learning to use magic. He'd made me repeat one particular rule every single night for a week until he'd been satisfied that I remembered it.

"Never draw on my own life force or the life force of others," I answered on autopilot.

He nodded. "Magic can be pulled from all living things – it's the very essence of nature. With the natural world now overrun by manmade technologies, it's likely that access to the land's magic will be impeded. There is one source, however, that will always remain accessible."

It took a moment before understanding dawned on me, and an inexplicable horror filled me. "You mean people."

He eyes darkened, but his expression remained shuttered. "There's a great deal of power held within the human life force. But access to it is volatile. The power is finite, and while it may convey a much-needed magic boost, that boost is temporary and the side effects are multiplied exponentially. That is why the rule is so important."

I wrapped my arms around myself, shivering despite the comfortable temperature that seemed to perpetually exist in the dreamscape. "Because it can result in death."

"Yes. Some can stop shy of draining the life force entirely, but it's a precarious knife-edge few would risk."

"Unless you didn't care about stopping because it's someone else's life force being drained."

"Exactly."

I dropped my head to my knees and squeezed my eyes closed. This was all my fault. Magic or no magic, the person behind this believed they would get power from these sacrifices – at least I assumed they did. So, even if, by some miracle, the magic didn't exist and this was all just a bad joke, my actions had set this in motion.

Killian allowed me a few moments with my thoughts before I felt the air stir as he rose to his feet. He held out a hand to me.

"We can't waste any more time. If somebody really is killing members of the Tuatha line to gather more magic, then you've got a very large target on your back. You need to be able to defend yourself – with magic."

I sighed, too weary to even argue. Instead, I accepted his offered hand and allowed him to tug me back up to standing. A thought occurred to me as I rose.

"Siobhán wrote a letter to me before she died. More like a blackmail note, actually. She said there's something wrong with Teagan and I'd need the Watchers of Danu if I wanted to help her. She implied it was something related to the magic."

He tilted his head, considering. "Teagan is the woman you live with?"

I nodded. "She wasn't well for a few days, but I can't see how it's connected. She collapsed when Siobhán was at the apartment, so more likely Siobhán was trying to –"

"Describe her symptoms to me," he said, cutting me off before I could continue my rambling justification.

I did, starting with the evening Teagan had returned from work upset, to her collapse the last time we'd seen Siobhán alive.

"You saw her eyes turn purple?"

"I think so. I mean, I can't be sure. It all happened so quickly."

"And Siobhán wrote the letter after her visit."

I nodded.

"So, she expected to die."

I considered that. "Her partner said she was going to follow up on a lead. I suppose it stands to reason that she might prepare for the worst."

"Or something else tipped her off," Killian said, as much to himself as to me. "Did your friend get any other bad news around the time she first seemed off?"

I began to shake my head but stopped, mentally slapping my forehead for forgetting. "One of her students was killed on her way home from the lecture. We don't know the exact details other than the fact she was murdered, but she had the same name as one of the victims that Siobhán mentioned. Teagan took it very hard, understandably, though I haven't mentioned the possible connection to her."

A strange look passed over Killian's face but he shut it down almost immediately, his expression once more unreadable as I was left wondering if I'd imagined it.

"What?" I demanded. "What is it?"

"I'm not sure." He turned away from me and I grabbed his shoulder to stop him.

"Tell me."

He turned back, reluctantly meeting my gaze, the sympathy once more a shadow behind his eyes. "I think it's possible your friend might be a banshee."

CHAPTER TEN

Try as I might, I couldn't focus on my work the next morning, and I passed the first couple of hours retyping a manuscript three times over thanks to my distraction.

Killian's words replayed on loop in my head. A banshee? How could Teagan be a banshee? That was ridiculous.

Even as I dismissed the idea, my mind kept jumping back to how upset she'd been returning from work on Friday. Sure, there could be a lot of innocent explanations for it, but less than twelve hours later, she'd gotten the call about her student.

Then there was Siobhán. Teagan had gotten the strangest expression on her face when she'd looked at Siobhán. I couldn't be completely sure if I'd seen her eyes change or if it had been my imagination, but I definitely remembered the blankness right before she collapsed. And less than twenty-four hours later, Siobhán had been murdered.

It had to be a coincidence. Didn't it?

The seed of doubt had been implanted, however, and try as I might to brush it off as crazy, I found little comfort in my denial.

Killian hadn't helped the situation either. After dropping the banshee bombshell, he'd been unhelpfully sparse with information. Apparently, banshees had been rare even in his time, with only certain family lines carrying the gene. He had, however, heard stories of people being driven mad by the ability to sense impending death. A fact that was not comforting in the slightest.

I didn't know a huge amount about Teagan's family. A history of addiction and mental abuse had led to her distancing herself from them as soon as she was old enough, and she didn't like to talk about them much. I was pretty sure she'd have told me if they were mythological beings, though.

The clock in the bottom corner of my computer screen informed me it was nearly lunchtime, a sentiment echoed by my rumbling stomach. I knew I should get out of the office for a bit to clear my head, but instead I clicked open a web browser. After a moment of hesitation, I typed the word "banshee".

I'd expected the number of results to be high, but my eyes bugged out when I saw the estimate of almost sixty-five million. I stared at the top results, chewing on my lip. Just like when I'd attempted to research the

Tuatha Dé Danann and the Fomorians a few weeks previous, I had no way of knowing what could be believed, so I picked a website at random, opened it, and scanned the text.

The myth of the banshee was well known in Ireland – the mysterious woman who combed her hair at your window and whose shriek foretold your death. The first couple of websites offered nothing new to the story, but the third included a note on the origin of the banshee, or *bean sídhe* as she was known in Gaeilge. Three words jumped out at me from the screen, three words I was quickly growing to hate: Tuatha Dé Danann.

Growling in frustration, I shut the web browser and lay my head down on the cool desk. What the hell was I going to do?

Siobhán had said the Watchers would help Teagan if I helped them. But would they? And what if I couldn't do what they wanted?

If I had the slightest idea how to stop the murders, I'd tell them in a heartbeat; nobody should ever have to die the way Siobhán did. The very fact that Brian thought I was purposely holding out on him was a joke. Did he really think that little of me?

Every minute I sat here clueless and inept was a minute more that Teagan could be suffering. Siobhán had said it would get worse. I couldn't just sit here twiddling –

"Aisling."

I jerked my head up in surprise, not having heard

my boss's approach. He had materialised next to me at some point during my mental debate. Thankfully, though, his attention seemed to be focused on his three companions rather than me, his paralegal, who looked suspiciously like she was having a nap on her desk.

It was the companion next to Clifford who caught my attention first. My breath hitched.

Declan Bannon.

Though I'd only met him once, there was no mistaking the pompous air that surrounded the head of the Order of the Fomori. He wore an expensive charcoal suit that made the grey dappling his black hair seem distinguished rather than ageing, and his steely grey eyes gave nothing away as they met mine.

He shifted slightly to the side, revealing a man that should have been instantly recognisable to me considering the countless hours I'd spent picturing his face on a dartboard while I decorated it with imaginary darts. As it was, I'd never in our previous encounters seen Bres so neatly turned out. My mouth fell open, and I was pretty sure a fly flew in before I managed to compose myself.

Bres's wavy blond locks were carefully styled and the tailored black suit perfectly accentuated his broad shoulders. He looked like he'd just stepped off the cover of *GQ* magazine. There was a familiar glint in those unforgettable blue eyes, and the lying, deceitful bastard even had the nerve to give me a cheeky wink.

"...make sure we're not disturbed."

I blinked. Clifford had continued talking while I'd

been caught up in my inner turmoil at seeing that treacherous fucker Bres again. Not waiting for a response from me, he indicated for his companions to follow him into the meeting room.

It was only as they retreated that I snapped out of my shock enough to turn my attention to the third man with them. He already had his back to me at that point, but there was something oddly familiar about the tall, stocky physique and shoulder-length black hair. Had I seen him when I'd been at the Order's headquarters?

The group disappeared behind the frosted glass walls of the meeting room and the door closed behind them. I blew out a shaky breath, my heart thudding in my chest as I turned back to my computer and attempted to get my shit together.

"We could do with more clients like that," Colette, one of the other paralegals noted with a chuckle, mistaking my reaction entirely. A weak smile was the only response I could muster.

What the hell was the Order doing here?

Of course I'd known they were clients of the firm. When Bres had been trying to get me onside, he'd staged a car crash and his own disappearance. I'd abused my position here at Smith & Mercer to obtain the address for the so-called secret organisation. That was when I'd had the pleasure of meeting Declan Bannon.

The head of the Order had agreed to help me find Bres, but only if I conducted their ritual. I'd stupidly done it, believing Bres to be a good guy instead of the dick he was.

Seeing members of the Order here now hit too close to home when I was already trying to deal with the fallout from my stupidity.

Any hope I had of concentrating on work for the rest of the afternoon was well and truly shot. No matter how much I tried, I couldn't shake my awareness of the meeting that was going on in the room mere feet from me. At least Clifford hadn't insisted that I sit in on it to take notes, as he often did.

By the time the door to the meeting room opened at five minutes to five, I had myself so keyed up that I almost leapt out of my seat. I felt Bres's presence at my shoulder a moment later, but I kept my gaze stubbornly fixed straight ahead on my screen.

"Can I help?" I ground out with saccharine sweetness.

He placed a hand on the back of my chair and bent over so that I could feel his warm breath tickle my ear. I forced myself not to cringe away.

"You already did," he replied, so quietly that only I could hear. "Now, let me help you. Know when to leave well enough alone. The murders aren't your problem. Don't draw any more attention to yourself than you already have."

I whipped my head around, all pretence of professionalism immediately forgotten. How did he know about the murders? Was the Order involved?

"Is that a threat?" I demanded, my tongue like sandpaper in my mouth.

Bres straightened and flashed me that familiar charming smile that made his eyes sparkle mischievously. "Not at all. Think of it more as friendly advice. I might have need of you in the future, and I'd rather you didn't go getting yourself killed."

Before I could answer, he turned and swanned out of the office, the eyes of every red-blooded female in the office following him as he did. If only they knew what that handsome façade hid.

A cool summer breeze ruffled my hair as I allowed myself to be swallowed up by the rush hour swarm that flooded the city centre. My mind was reeling. Bres, the Order, sacrifices, all of it consumed me until it felt like my head would explode.

I had no love for the Order, and I was under no illusions that they were above breaking the law. But murder? Surely even they wouldn't stoop to something so heinous. Besides, what could they hope to achieve from it? It made no sense.

Maybe Bres was just fucking with me? It was the kind of thing he'd likely get a kick out of.

Seeing him again had shaken me more than I wanted to admit. The realisation that he could still get under my skin pissed me off and left me feeling raw in a way I wasn't equipped to deal with right now. No doubt he was laughing at my expense.

I'd scarpered from the office before Bannon emerged from the meeting room, not wanting to face a second run-in with the head of the Order as well. Was it cowardly? Probably, but I needed some air. Not to mention headspace to consider Bres's warning.

As I made my way further out of the city, the crowd around me began to thin. Commuters bustled for a spot on their public transport of choice, and the drone of conversation faded to be replaced by the steady hum of traffic. I focused on the sounds, trying to quieten the questions that kept buzzing around my head.

What had the Order been doing at Smith & Mercer? How had Bres known about the murders – or my involvement, for that matter?

The clever thing to do would be to tell Brian what had happened and let him deal with it. But what if Bres really was just trying to mess with my head? The Watcher hated the Order; that much had been clear from the moment I'd met him. Would he be capable of staying partial? Or would he let his hatred cloud his judgement and condemn them without a proper investigation?

As if my very thoughts had drawn his attention, my phone started buzzing. I pulled it out of my bag, and my steps faltered as I saw Brian's name flashing up at me. The insistent vibration demanded that I make a decision. My finger hovered over the screen.

If I answered, I'd have to tell him what Bres said.

There was no way I could hide the fact that something was wrong, not with how I was feeling right now. Every instinct I had was warning me to proceed carefully, however.

The Watchers and the Order had a history that I'd only scratched the surface of, and stirring up trouble between the two when I had nothing solid to go on seemed like a very bad idea. I had to be sure before I voiced my concerns and opened a can of worms that couldn't be closed again. No more rash decisions. Not when there was so much at stake.

Hoping I was doing the right thing, I slid the phone back into my bag. I'd speak to Brian when I got home; I just needed a bit more time to think.

Pete hadn't contacted me after my visit the day before, and I'd been unable to shake the niggle of concern that plagued the back of my mind despite more recent distractions. I wanted to check on him again, if only to put one of my many worries to rest, and figured now was as good a time as any.

Veering away from the harsh grey of the city towards the Phoenix Park, I allowed the wide expanse of green to beckon me forward. Joggers overtook me on the path, absorbed by the meditative rhythm of their footfall, while mothers pushed buggies and called for their older children not to stray too far away on their bikes. It was all so normal.

Where had I gone wrong? Between sacrificial murders, my best friend possibly being a harbinger of death, and an errant ex-boyfriend, I couldn't remember the last time my life had been filled with such mundane things. A pang of jealousy stirred in my chest.

Irritated at myself for the petty feeling, I turned left down a tree-lined path and away from all the happy, normal people.

I hadn't gone far when a strange prickle ran down the back of my neck. I looked around nervously.

There was no sign of another person nearby, but I couldn't shake the feeling that somebody was watching me. It was the same eerie feeling I'd gotten at Pete's house the day before, and suddenly, being alone didn't seem like such a great idea.

Quickening my pace, I mentally mapped out where the closest exit was that would lead me back out onto the main road. I'd only gone a short distance when I heard it. A low, menacing growl.

CHAPTER ELEVEN

Every muscle in my body tensed in terror, my instincts screaming at me in warning. Slowly, I turned towards the tree line, my breath frozen in my chest. Yellow eyes glowed back at me from the shadows.

A large dog with dark brown fur stepped out from the trees. *It looks like a wolf*, I mused, the thought tinged with a vague sense of panic. But that couldn't be possible – there weren't any wolves in Ireland.

Except there were, I remembered numbly. Dublin Zoo was situated in the heart of the Phoenix Park, not far from where I stood now. It housed many animals not native to these lands, and wolves were on that list.

My mouth went dry as adrenaline shot through my veins. Had this creature escaped from the zoo? I was filled with the urge to turn and flee. But could I outrun the animal?

About ready to piss myself with fear, I inched backwards, not taking my eyes off the wolf for a second. It let out a low, warning growl and bared razor-sharp fangs.

The sight of those terrifying large teeth spurred me into motion. I spun on my heel, preparing to run faster than I ever had in my life. Instead, I hit a solid wall of muscle.

A hand clamped over my mouth, smothering the scream that tried to break free from my throat.

My eyes – the only part of me that could still move – travelled up a broad chest to land on a face shrouded in shadow beneath the hood of a black leather coat. The form was distinctly masculine and strangely familiar, but the more I tried to focus on my assailant's features, the more the shadows swirled and a thick murkiness filled my head.

An arm snaked around my waist, pinning me closer to the man. Not that it was required because his piercing gaze held me frozen as sure as his grip did. Some distant part of my mind warned that I should be very afraid, but every time I tried to focus on the thought, a thick fog of confusion filled my head.

A snarl from behind snapped my thoughts back into crystal clear focus and sent a bolt of fear shooting through me. I registered the hand covering my mouth and the arm pinning me tight, and a scream bubbled up in my throat, unable to break free.

The man's grip loosened abruptly as he shifted his

attention to something over my shoulder. He shoved me to the side, and I hit the pavement with a jarring thud that sent a flash of pain through my shoulder.

Rolling onto my back, I let loose my scream as the wolf leapt over my head and collided with my assailant.

The scene turned into a terrifying blur of claws, limbs, and teeth that sent me scrambling backwards, desperate to put as much space between myself and the fight as I could. Still, my eyes remained riveted as vicious fangs snapped at the man's neck.

With a snarl of his own, the man grabbed the wolf's forelegs. He gave a wrenching twist and flung the creature at a nearby tree. There was a loud crack and a pained yelp as the wolf slid to the ground. I covered my mouth in horror.

It lay there unmoving for the longest time. Fear of the animal turned to fear for the animal, and my heart stuttered in my chest as I willed it to get up.

Suddenly, it jumped to its feet. With a brisk shake, it stood to attention and bared its teeth once more.

Relief shuddered through me, only to be replaced an instant later by panic.

I jerked my head around in search of the man in shadows. He was gone.

Heart racing, I scoured the shadows cast by the trees lining the road. Where was he? He couldn't have just disappeared.

The wolf, too, seemed to scan the area. When no further attacks were forthcoming, the tension left its body and it slumped to the ground once more. I eyed it nervously, acutely aware that this wild animal could turn on me at any moment. Yet, as crazy as the thought was, I couldn't shake the feeling that the wolf had saved me. I couldn't just leave it here if it was injured.

Slowly, and with my eyes watching for even the slightest twitch or sign of aggression from the animal, I rose to my feet. Pain lanced through my side, but I fought to keep my breathing calm as I inched closer to where it lay.

Dogs could sense fear. Was that the same for wolves? I had no bloody idea, but just in case, I tried to imagine it as a cute, friendly puppy. Nothing to be afraid of here.

Yellow eyes watched me as I moved, and I could've sworn a spark of recognition shone in them.

"Are you hurt?" I asked, though what response I was expecting I had no idea.

I stopped at what I thought to be a safe distance away and considered my options. I couldn't just leave it here like this. Maybe if I rang the zoo, they could send someone to retrieve their missing animal?

The wolf shifted and I took an involuntary step backwards. More slowly, almost as if it was trying not to spook me, it rose to its feet. One leg buckled slightly as it did.

Shit, it was hurt.

Regaining its balance, the wolf gave me a long look, then turned and made its way towards the cover of the trees. A sane person would have let it go and breathed a sigh of relief over surviving the encounter without being eaten. Me? I hesitated for a second to acknowledge my stupidity, then followed.

As I did, I pulled my phone from my bag. I might be stupid, but I could at least contact the zoo while I was doing it.

Just as I got it unlocked and ready to search for a phone number, something caught my attention in the overgrowth among the trees. The wolf headed straight for it, but I froze, my unconscious brain registering the shape as a body before my eyes could catch up and translate the image for the rest of me.

Oh, hell no. Not again.

My palms grew sweaty and my stomach flipped as I noted with a mild sense of hysteria that the person wasn't moving. I'd already seen one dead body, and that was one too many to last a lifetime as far as I was concerned; I wasn't sure I could face another one.

As if realising I was no longer following, the wolf turned and looked back at me expectantly.

My feet were rooted to the ground and I was frozen with indecision. Move forward and possibly lose what was left of my sanity? Or flee like a coward and risk leaving someone that needed help with a wild animal I knew nothing about?

Really, there was no choice. So, with great effort, I forced my feet to move again. The shape grew more distinct as I got closer. Whoever it was lay with their back to me, but the form appeared to be male. Leaves were tangled in the short brown hair and there were grass stains on the grey hooded sweatshirt. It could be a homeless person sleeping rough, though based on the brand name trainers I didn't think so.

"Hello," I called in a half whisper. "Are you okay?"

Silence mocked me for the idiotic question.

I was trying to recall any of my past first aid training when the wolf stepped closer to the man. Visions of the animal chomping on flesh instantly flooded my mind, and I reached out in a panic, as if that simple gesture could stop it from happening.

The wolf didn't move to bite the man, however. Rather, it stepped into the space where the man lay and seemed to simply disappear. There was a low groan and the body stirred.

I gasped, stumbling backwards.

Leaves crunched beneath my feet as I did, and the sound caused the man to whip his head around in my direction. Familiar brown eyes met mine, and my hands flew to my mouth in shock.

Pete, my ex-boyfriend, eyed me warily from where he remained, half lying on the ground. He held perfectly still, as if afraid that even the slightest twitch might spook me. His skin was pale, but I could see no obvious signs of injury. And what's more, I could see no sign of the creature that had only minutes ago saved me.

I blinked dumbly at him as my brain scrambled to make sense of what I was seeing. Had I simply been hallucinating? That didn't make sense; if I'd imagined the wolf, then I had to have imagined the man in shadows too. That was a whole lot of crazy, even for me.

"Pete?" I squeaked, as if saying his name would clarify things. Maybe it was him I was hallucinating?

"Hey, Aisling."

Nope. Definitely not hallucinating.

CHAPTER TWELVE

I stared at Pete over the steaming cup of chamomile tea that rested on the table in front of me. We'd found a quiet corner upstairs in the Phoenix Park Café, but even with the relative privacy I was at a loss for where to start.

My ex looked just as he always had, yet there was something different about him, something wilder. His dark brown hair had always been a bit too long to be considered neat, but now it looked unkempt. The sparkle normally present in his brown eyes was replaced with a weary watchfulness. His glasses too were gone, and I idly wondered if he'd started wearing contact lenses.

The cup of sugary tea I'd ordered for him sat on the table, untouched. He'd all but inhaled the selection of pastries I'd bought, though; it appeared his adventures in the park had left him hungry.

"Your mam is worried about you," I said, the fact

that she clearly had a reason to be hanging unspoken in the air.

Pete let out a soft snort but didn't respond.

The awkward tension between us was new and uncomfortable. We'd always been able to talk freely to each other. Right up to the end of our relationship, Pete had been one of my best friends and closest confidantes. It had been the main reason I'd found it so hard to admit to myself that I didn't really love him the same way he loved me. Now, it felt like I was sitting across from a stranger.

"Talk to me." I reached across the table for his hand, but he pulled it back out of reach.

He looked me in the eye just long enough for me to see the flash of vulnerability before looking away once more.

"I came to see you yesterday," I pressed, ignoring the sting of hurt I felt at him flinching from my touch.

"I know."

So, he had been home. I bloody knew it.

"You didn't answer." No response. "What were you doing in the trees?"

"I don't know."

"Did it have anything to do with the wolf?"

He stilled. The energy around him was suddenly charged, and my instinctive need to flee kicked in again. But I held my ground.

For a long time he didn't say anything, and I wondered if I was wasting my time. Then he looked at me with a defiant expression.

"It was worried."

It? Were we still talking about the wolf?

"About what?" I asked, careful to keep my tone casual and relaxed despite the questions whirring around my mind.

"You."

"The wolf was worried about me?"

A faint blush crept up his cheeks, and he nodded.

"Why was the wolf worried about me?"

Memories flashed into my mind of those dark, piercing eyes and the shadows they hid behind. Even as the image came, it dissipated, that strange murkiness making it difficult to grasp the thought that was hovering just beyond my reach.

The wolf had growled only seconds before the man grabbed me. I'd assumed the creature was growling at me, but it had bypassed me entirely and gone for my assailant. If it hadn't been for the wolf, who knew what would've happened? I shuddered.

Pete opened his mouth to answer, then seemed to think better of it. He shook his head, slumping back into his chair in resignation. "You wouldn't believe me."

I let a wry laugh. "You'd be surprised. Try me."

Still, he hesitated. "When you came to the house yesterday it ... sensed danger around you. So, we – I – followed you."

Not sure what to make of that, I pressed on. "Where's the wolf now?"

"Inside me."

The words were spoken so softly that I wasn't quite

sure if I'd heard them right, but the defeated way Pete hung his head told me I had. *Holy shit!*

"What do you mean inside you?"

"I don't know." He slammed his hand down on the table and let out a growl of frustration. Liquid sloshed from the untouched cup of tea, and wary eyes turned to watch us from the few occupied tables that surrounded us.

Cheeks reddening once more, Pete yanked some napkins out of the metal holder and set about mopping up the tea from the table.

"I don't know how to explain it," he admitted, looking so forlorn that I wanted to wrap my arms around him. "I can feel it. Inside of me. It watches, senses things I can't see. It sees the people that need protecting, and it protects them."

This was not how I expected the conversation to go. Even with the magic and sacrifices that had apparently become the norm in my life in recent weeks, I was at a complete loss as to what to say. So, I shifted back to safer ground while I tried to make sense of what he was telling me.

"Thank you. For saving me in the park."

Pete's eyes flashed yellow for a second, and my breath caught as I glimpsed the wolf behind them. They returned to their normal shade almost immediately, but I couldn't shake the sense that the wolf was watching.

"That man was going to hurt you."

I swallowed the lump in my throat at the unwelcome reminder. "I think so."

He nodded, as if that fact allowed everything else to make sense. But it didn't make sense; none of this did.

Pete and I had been together for three years. We'd lived together for more than half of that. How had I never noticed that he had a freaking wolf inside him?

Just as quickly as the question came into my mind, another thought occurred to me. I froze, horror dawning on me.

"Pete, how long has the wolf been around?"

His mother said he'd only started acting strange a few weeks ago. Before that, I'd never known him to be anything other than a nice, normal guy. He'd always been protective of the people he cared about, but he was never one to don a superhero cape and rush into potentially deadly situations to save the day.

"About a month, I guess. Not long after I saw you last, I started having blackouts. I'd wake up in random places, not able to remember what had happened. I thought it was stress, what with..." He gave an apologetic shrug towards me.

"Over time, I was more ... aware of when it was likely to happen. Something would make me angry and I wouldn't be able to control it. There would be this overwhelming need to protect, to make things right. The wolf's need. Sometimes I get flashbacks afterwards, but it's like I'm watching through someone else's eyes."

"That's why you shut yourself away from everyone,"

I said, the sinking realisation settling like lead in my gut.

He looked up at me, eyes wide and full of fear. "I don't want to hurt anyone."

<hr>

Pete was quiet on the taxi ride back to his house. I forced a mumbled agreement from him to call me if he needed anything and watched him trudge up the drive-way, hands in his pockets, head hung low. Though it appeared I'd unravelled the mystery that had Pete's mother so worried, I had absolutely no idea what I could say to the woman to put her mind at ease, given what I now knew. So, I did what any self-respecting adult would do and put it into the column of things to be dealt with later.

My head was pounding by the time I reached the apartment. Any adrenaline had long since left my system, and my hand was trembling as I pressed the button for the lift.

It had finally struck me on the drive home just why my assailant seemed so familiar. I'd seen him before – as I was leaving St. Stephen's Green park.

Now that I remembered, I couldn't understand how I'd forgotten in the first place. How had the creepy guy in shadows not seemed out of place at a crime scene? And why did my head go all funny any time I thought about him?

I needed to call Brian and tell him what I knew.

Unlocking the apartment door, I flicked on the apartment lights. Teagan wasn't due back from work for a while, so it would give me time to get my thoughts straight and talk to the Watcher.

I stopped in surprise.

The rose that had been waiting outside the apartment for me the day before now occupied a vase in the centre of the kitchen table. I knew I'd left it in the box, my head too occupied to worry about keeping the thing alive. Perhaps Teagan had found it and decided to save it from dying of dehydration?

An uncomfortable sensation tap-danced down my spine, and I eyed the rose warily, feeling uneasy all of a sudden. Maybe it was because I never thanked the sender?

I'd been in a rush to get to work early this morning to make up for yesterday's tardiness, so I hadn't had a chance to ask Teagan if she knew who dropped it off. Dothur was the obvious assumption, but now that I thought of it, how would he have gotten my address?

As I looked again at the flower's silky petals, their unusually dark colour suddenly felt more ominous than romantic. I knew it was likely an aftereffect of what happened in the park and it was stupid to project my residual fear onto an inanimate object, but I couldn't shake the feeling.

Before I could second-guess myself and let paranoia take hold, I pulled out my phone and typed a message to Dothur.

Is it you that I should thank for the rose?

I chewed on my lip as I stared at the phone, waiting for a response. There'd be a simple explanation as to how he got my address, and I'd feel like an idiot for letting the nice gesture put me on edge.

Despite my best intentions, memories of those piercing eyes and swirling shadows assailed me. The phone vibrated and I jumped, almost dropping it. It took me a moment to calm my racing heart enough to realise it was Dothur responding to my message.

I'm afraid not. However, I would most like to take you out again so that I may rectify my oversight.

My stomach dropped. If the rose hadn't been from him, who was it from? And how the hell had they found out where I lived, not to mention gotten through the main security gates to leave it at the door?

Once more, memories of the attack came back to me, and a chill settled in the centre of my chest.

Despite it still being light out, I was unable to properly remember my assailant's face. Even as his eyes had held me transfixed, the shadows had ensured his features remained obscured. There was no doubt in my mind, however, that it was the same man I'd bumped into when fleeing from Siobhán's lifeless body.

Didn't they say that killers often liked to stick around the scene of their crimes to watch the after-effect?

My hand was shaking so badly that it took me three attempts to pull out my phone and scroll to the list of recent calls. I hit redial on the most recent missed call.

"You were meant to ring me yesterday," Brian answered, clearly too pissed to bother with the normal civilised greetings.

"Something came up." My voice sounded strangely hollow to my ears, and I numbly wondered if shock had finally set in at just how insane my life had gotten. "I have a possible lead for you."

"I'm coming over."

"No," I said firmly. "I will tell you over the phone, but first you need to do something for me."

"You know the deal. The Watchers aren't helping you with your friend's problem until you help us with ours."

"That's not what I'm asking." I'd known already that it would be pointless to waste my breath. "All I need is a yes or no answer, then I'll tell you what I know."

He growled in irritation. "Fine."

"Is Teagan a banshee?"

The pause that followed was so long that I actually checked my phone to make sure the call hadn't disconnected. After what seemed like an eternity, he sighed.

"Yes."

CHAPTER THIRTEEN

"I'm ready to learn."

The dreamscape had barely materialised around me before the words left my mouth. And for the first time since this whole mess had begun, I truly meant them.

Rather than rejoicing at my newfound compliance and launching straight into the lesson, Killian eyed me warily. "What happened?"

"What do you know about wolves?"

He raised an eyebrow in what I took to be surprise, but considered my question. "I know they're a subspecies of Canis lupus. The grey wolf was around in my time, but I believe they're no longer found in the wild in Ireland. Human developments come with a cost, and it's not always the humans that pay it."

"What about ones that live inside people?"

This time there was no mistaking his surprise. His eyes widened and he grew so still that it almost seemed as though he'd been frozen. I had a moment to muse on the fact that I seemed to be taking him off guard a lot lately. Go me.

"You mean a werewolf."

I shook my head firmly. "No. We are not just going to throw that word around. I'm talking about a normal, everyday wolf, not some abomination from a horror movie. This one just happens to reside inside a human. One minute it was there, the next it disappeared."

"And was there an unconscious person nearby?"

I nodded.

"Werewolf," he repeated. "I don't know what abominations you're referring to – or what a movie is, for that matter – but what you're describing sounds exactly like an Irish werewolf."

"Wait – you don't know what a movie is?" My brain glitched on that part of his comment, forgetting about the wolf issue for a second.

With his modern appearance and how au fait he seemed to be with the world as it was today, I often forgot that Killian came from a time I couldn't even imagine. He'd told me once that he'd volunteered for the role of dream mentor as his skills as a dream walker made him the best candidate, but any time I asked why, he changed the subject. Whenever I stopped to really think what that sacrifice meant for him, it hurt my head, and my heart. Millennia held in stasis. Had he been aware? What must it have been like for him to wake up with the world changed so drastically?

"Why are you asking about werewolves?" he pressed, ignoring my question.

I dropped my head in my hands and groaned. "It looks like my ex-boyfriend might be one. And it's all my fault."

He snorted – actually snorted – and I looked up at him in shock. Killian was the epitome of calm and collected, yet I'd made him snort. I was breaking all kinds of records lately.

But as satisfying as it was to break through that stoic exterior, I didn't have the time to be giving myself pats on the back; I needed information if I was going to help my friends, and I needed it before fate decided to spring any more fun surprises on me. So, I brought him up to speed on the events of the day, leading to my discovery of Pete's new, and slightly furrier, nature.

"You didn't make your ex a werewolf," he said when I'd finally finished. "He always was one. That part of his genetics was just dormant while the magic was held at bay."

"Yeah, yeah. Just like Teagan was always a banshee. Problem is, they were both happy while the magic was locked away. Now, thanks to me, they have this whole new side to them that they'll have to deal with, and it's going to make their lives miserable."

"Trying to be something other than what we are often does that to us," Killian said softly. He straightened, his demeanour instantly returning to one of business. "You say shadows surrounded the man who attacked you?"

I nodded. A shiver ran down my spine despite the warm summer day that seemed to be a constant in this place. "It was weird. I tried to see his face, but the shadows kept shifting and obscuring his features. Everything except his eyes. His eyes were piercing. They sucked you in and..."

Killian's jaw tightened almost imperceptibly, but I immediately knew that something about the description rang a bell with him.

"You know who it is," I said, the words almost an accusation.

"Maybe."

I crossed my arms and stubbornly waited.

"A very long time ago, three brothers came to Ireland with their mother, a powerful witch called Carmen. They came with the intention of conquering the land, and everywhere they went, plague and death followed in their wake. The Tuatha Dé Danann eventually stopped them, but not without great cost."

"How did they do it?" I asked, curious.

"One of our most talented mages managed to nullify their magic long enough for us to defeat them. Carmen was bound and imprisoned, and her three sons were banished from this land, never to return so long as water doth surround it."

I frowned. "Which it still does last I checked. Besides, if what you're talking about happened thousands of years ago, how could it possibly relate to my attack?"

"Like I said, Carmen was a powerful witch. History

books will tell you she died of a broken heart after being imprisoned here in Ireland, separated from her sons. The truth is that when the Tuatha sacrificed themselves to rid the land of magic, it cut her off from the source of her magic too. And as a consequence, the source of her immortality. Without it, she began to age once more. But instead of succumbing to the ravages of old age, she killed herself so that her essence would be preserved to one day exact revenge on those who'd imprisoned her.

"Her sons returned to their homeland, and unless the magic of that land was similarly impeded, it would be prudent to assume that they retained their immortality."

I stared at him, my brain feeling like it might actually split in two if I was expected to be any more open-minded. Magic had been hard enough to process. Now I was throwing banshees, werewolves, and immortal witches into the mix; it was getting beyond ridiculous.

"So, what? You think it was one of the sons of Carmen who attacked me?"

"I'm saying it's possible." There was that subtle clenching of his jaw again. "The sons were known by many names, but in English their names loosely translated as Darkness, Evil, and Violence. Darkness's power lay in shadows. He could wield them, turn them into a tangible force to confuse and disorientate his opponent."

Just like my attacker had.

I wrapped my arms tighter around my midsection

and muttered, "They sound like a bloody cheap version of the horsemen of the apocalypse."

"That wouldn't be an unfair comment. Compared to their mother, the sons were low-level magic users. But when all four worked together, they caused much damage and destruction before they were stopped."

His grim tone and earlier words told me that he'd borne witness to at least some of that devastation, and I itched to pry further. But there'd be time for that later. Now, I needed to figure out what the hell all this meant for my current situation.

"Okay. Let's say the sons – or one of them at least – are still alive. I go back to my point about Ireland being an island. I know I messed up with the whole releasing magic thing, but there's no way I'm taking responsibility for drying up the sea."

Killian's lip twitched, and for a whole second, I thought he might even smile. "No, you're correct. You do still live on an island. But we have no way of knowing how the removal and subsequent return of magic affected the curse that was placed on them."

"Why would they wait so long to come back then?"

"When they were banished, they swore revenge against the Tuatha. The return of magic would provide them an avenue to exact that revenge from a position of strength. I can only assume it acted as the catalyst."

Well, shit. Yet another fun side effect of my screw-up. What next? Were puppies and chocolate going to suddenly cease to exist?

Despair weighed heavily on me as I considered this

new information and what it might mean for my deal with the Watchers. They wanted me to help stop the sacrifices, but even if this whole magic crap did suddenly click for me, I didn't fancy my chances against an immortal with thousands of years' worth of experience – let alone three of them.

"There's something else you should know."

I closed my eyes and groaned, Killian's tone telling me I wouldn't like what came next. Maybe I could wake myself up from the dream and go find a nice sandpit to bury my head in again? Instead, I heaved a sigh and opened my eyes to look at him.

"The mage that nullified the powers of Carmen and her sons, she was your ancestor. It was from her that the Guardian line was created."

I sucked in a breath. Godammit, why did my ancestors have to get themselves mixed up in this shite? Could they not have been lowly farmers who minded their own business and worried only about what the next crop would yield?

I allowed myself a couple of minutes to wallow, but ultimately it was pointless. So I squared my shoulders and strengthened my resolve. "Well, I'm not her. But I do have friends to help, so let's get to work."

CHAPTER FOURTEEN

How was it possible to be exhausted while you were sleeping? Every part of my body felt heavy and sweat ran in rivulets down the back of my neck. Killian had taken me at my word that I was ready to get serious about my training and had been pushing me relentlessly for what seemed like hours.

"Again," he demanded.

"I really don't understand how this is going to help me." Panting, I doubled over to place my hands on my knees. I was pretty sure that if I had to run another lap of the meadow, I'd keel over and die of a heart attack.

"We've tried the meditation and it hasn't worked. Your mental blocks are too firmly in place, and they're stopping you from accessing the magic while you have the ability to overthink. So, we're taking away that ability."

"By killing me?"

His eyes sparkled with amusement. "By tiring you

out and giving your mind something else to focus on. Now, again."

I groaned but turned on my heel and sluggishly forced my feet to get moving. Every footfall was heavier than the last, every breath more laboured. This time when I returned to his side I sprawled on the ground, and nothing he said was going to get me up again.

Seemingly satisfied that he'd broken me to a sufficient degree, Killian nodded. "Okay, close your eyes."

With pleasure.

"Sink into the ground. Feel its energy."

It didn't take any thought on my part to follow his instructions this time. My body was so grateful to be horizontal that I gladly embraced the ground's hold on me. My own energy was so depleted that even the blade of grass tickling my hand felt like it had more energy than I did.

"Let that energy absorb into you. Let it settle at your core. Allow it to build."

I let my mind drift as his words wrapped around me. A strange sensation blossomed to life at my centre below my naval. It was foreign and yet oddly familiar. But it remained just out of reach.

There was a vague rustling beside me, and I became acutely aware of Killian's warmth as he crouched down next to me.

My breath caught as I felt his hands rest gently on my shoulders. Every part of my awareness heightened until I could focus on nothing else aside from his touch. A spark of electricity shot through me, and suddenly there it was.

The magic.

I tried in vain to concentrate on the report I was typing up for Clifford, but my mind kept wandering back to my training with Killian, and my hand kept drifting to rest on my lower abdomen.

I could hardly believe what I'd felt. Even now in my waking hours, I was aware of a low hum that buzzed just under the surface. It was nothing like the surge of power when Killian touched me, but I couldn't deny its presence.

The threads of magic were there, teasing me with the vibrant possibilities that were almost within my reach. Pens were lying around just waiting to be floated.

Of course, it remained to be seen what that magic would allow me to do. Killian had once explained that each person had a natural affinity which would shape their use of energy. Tapping into it was just the first step. Now, I needed to figure out how to use it.

Staring at the litany of legal jargon on the screen in front of me, I cursed the fact that I was a grownup and had to sit here pretending to be interested in this stupid job when all I really wanted to do was further explore my potential.

As pleased as I was with my breakthrough,

however, my mood had quickly soured when I woke this morning and remembered the threat that loomed in the shadows. I'd tried to call Brian to talk to him about Killian's theory regarding the sons of Carmen. He'd cancelled the call and sent an abrupt message to inform me he wasn't free to talk, but I was to meet him after work at a nearby pub.

It was only afterwards that I realised it was probably a good thing he hadn't answered. I needed time to think of a plausible explanation for where the information had come from, since I wasn't planning on telling him – and, by extension, the Watchers – about Killian.

Glancing at the clock, I started. I was due in a meeting in less than fifteen minutes and I really needed to get my head out of my arse.

Hurriedly, I transcribed the last of Clifford's near indecipherable notes and hit Send. He'd told me to make sure I put the good biscuits out for the meeting, so I had to assume the client was someone important; it made no difference to me, however, since I was just there to take notes.

I managed to prepare the meeting room and get myself settled, somewhat breathless, in the corner of the spacious room just in time. Voices drifted to me from the main office, and I had a moment for realisation to settle like a brick in my stomach before Bres walked through the frosted glass door.

Decked out in a light grey suit that conveniently hid his metaphorical devil horns and forked tail, he met my gobsmacked gaze and gave me a conspiratorial wink.

My boss appeared behind him before I could speak. "Ah, Aisling, you're here. Good."

I shut my gaping mouth with a snap and fixed a professional smile on my face as another man followed Clifford into the room.

The man's broad shoulders strained against the seams of his black shirt as he settled into one of the leather chairs that surrounded the large oak table. His shoulder-length black hair was tied into a ponytail at the base of his neck, allowing me a clear view of his tanned features, complete with a strong jaw coated in a light stubble.

This was the man who had attended the previous meeting with the Order. At the time, I'd been so thrown by seeing Bannon and Bres again that I hadn't paid him much heed. As I saw him now, I instantly realised what had triggered that vague spark of recognition. He was the man who had been arguing with Dothur as I'd arrived for our date.

As if sensing my attention, he turned his dark gaze on me. A harsh fire blazed behind his eyes, and I shivered, my throat constricting.

Dothur hadn't specifically said that the man he'd been arguing with was his brother, though he had implied they were family. Now that I had a proper view of the man, it was hard to deny the resemblance between the two.

Questions whirred through my head as Clifford

closed the door to the meeting room and joined the other two men around the table. I held my hands stiffly over my laptop, muscle memory taking over despite my distraction.

"I have the final paperwork here for you to sign, Mr. Athanosios." Clifford placed a folder in front of the dark-haired man and indicated to the pages marked with colourful sticky tabs.

My breath caught at the confirmation that the man was indeed related to Dothur. What business did he have with the Order? And more to the point, was Dothur involved too?

The conversation continued with no regard to my inner turmoil. Little of what they said made sense to me as Bres and the other man, who I learned was called Dain, hammered out some final terms around a new form of natural energy Dain and his partners were working on. It was only as Clifford finally started to wind up the meeting that something penetrated the fog of confusion I'd found myself in.

"That's settled then. Carmen Holdings will officially transfer ownership to you and your brothers on successful completion of the deal at midnight on 31st July."

My blood ran cold.

How many brothers had Dothur said he had?

CHAPTER FIFTEEN

I took my time tidying up after the meeting, still trying to process the maelstrom of questions and emotions that had resulted from my sinking realisation. Of course, it made sense that someone as handsome and successful as Dothur would be too good to be true, but I still couldn't get my head around the possibility that he might somehow be mixed up in this whole mess.

Both Dain and Bres left the meeting without acknowledging me, and the tension that had held my muscles in a vice for the past hour eased marginally. With the breathing space came a curiosity that I couldn't quite quash, however.

I turned to Clifford, who sat checking his emails, as oblivious as ever. "If you don't need me for anything else right now, I'll grab an early lunch?"

He dismissed me with a wave of his hand, and I hurried to grab my bag from the main office.

I wasn't sure if I was relieved or not when I made it down to the main reception on the ground floor and spotted Dain and Bres speaking just beyond the glass doors of the building. Something about how they faced off with each other made me feel there was an underlying animosity that had been carefully concealed in the meeting, but I was too far away to have any hope of overhearing their conversation.

Thinking inconspicuous thoughts, I pretended to search for something in my bag, all the while moving slowly towards the door and keeping the two men in my sights. Apparently done with their conversation, they departed in opposite directions. I stared after Bres for a long moment before I darted out the door and followed Dain.

At just a little past noon, the city was already bustling with people eager to beat the lunch hour rush, which made it easy for me to blend into the crowd. Still, my heart was pounding as I waited for him to turn around at any second and spot me. When he veered right down a narrow side street, I hesitated.

What was I doing? This man could very well be dangerous if I was right about who he was. I had to be crazy to think this was a good idea. Still, I had to be sure.

He had almost disappeared completely from my eyeline before I made my decision. Chest tight with the breath I was half afraid to release, I gave one final glance around before following.

The buildings that bordered either side of the street

cast shadows that afforded some meagre cover, but aside from the odd skip or bin that could shield me, I was hyper-aware of just how exposed I was. Thankfully, Dain seemed focused only on his destination as he made his way through a winding pattern of twists and turns at a brisk pace.

I kept as much distance between us as I could without losing sight of him entirely. He disappeared around a corner and I slowed my pace.

Was it a trap? Had he known I was following him all along and he was waiting now to jump out at me? My heart raced and I licked my dry lips as I considered whether to turn back.

"Is it done?"

I bit back a scream as the low-spoken words reached me from around the corner. It wasn't Dain's voice, but it sent a shiver of recognition through me, nonetheless. Recognition and terror.

"Yes," Dain snapped from where he remained out of sight. "Everything is in place, so it's time you stop fucking about. We only have two more to go to fulfil our side of the deal. Forget about your new little obsession and get your head in the game because if you mess this up, we won't get another chance."

"I'm well aware of what's at stake."

"Are you? It seems like I'm the only one who actually remembers why we're here."

"Don't you dare..."

The whispered threat slithered over my skin, and

even though it wasn't aimed at me, it froze me to the spot in terror. That voice... Oh god, that voice.

My pulse thundered in my ears so loudly that I was convinced the men on the other side of the wall would hear it at any minute and become aware of my presence. I needed to get out of here, but I couldn't go without knowing I was right, without knowing who the man was that Dain was arguing with.

Legs trembling, I crouched low and inched towards the corner. With my breath held, I peered around the jagged brick edge of the building, ready to bolt at the slightest indication that I'd been caught.

The first thing I saw was Dain. He was standing with his back to me in a narrow alley, his broad frame blocking the second man from my view. Then he shifted, gesturing in clear agitation, and I saw him. The man in shadows.

I stumbled back, swallowing the gasp that tried to involuntarily escape at seeing my attacker.

A warm hand clamped over my mouth and I was yanked to my feet. "I told you to keep your nose out of this."

CHAPTER SIXTEEN

A jolt of energy flared to life within my core as fright allowed me to instinctively tap into the tenuous thread of magic that remained there. But before I could even think of using it, it sputtered and died just like the scream that froze in my throat. The sudden silence that fell on the other side of the wall halted any desire I had to struggle.

Bres kept his hand firmly clamped over my mouth as he twisted me around to face him. The curiosity that glinted in his assessing gaze was replaced by a grim expression as he looked towards the unseen alley. He held a finger to his lips in warning and flicked his eyes back in the direction from which I'd come.

I nodded my understanding.

Tentatively, I edged back down the narrow side street, allowing him to lead me for fear that my legs might give out from under me. As we neared the main street, he finally released the clamp on my mouth and switched instead to a light grip on my arm. I risked a quick glance behind me, but the path was empty.

"Are you following me?" I hissed.

He raised an eyebrow, his blue eyes sparkling with mirth as the tension eased from his face. "That's rich. Do you often pass your lunch hour wandering around random side streets?"

I glared at him in response.

"Come on." He chuckled. "I'll buy you a coffee."

Despite my better judgement, my feet followed him. Clearly I must have been in a state of shock because the last thing I wanted to do was humour this man; knowing him, the coffee would likely be poisoned. And yet, somehow, I found myself a few minutes later seated across from him in the coffee shop next to Smith & Mercer.

I refused to answer him when he asked me my drink of choice, stubbornly crossing my arms in a somewhat pathetic act of protest. Whether or not I managed to hide my look of surprise when he placed a hot chocolate in front of me, I wasn't sure, but he reeked of smug satisfaction as he grinned at me.

"Thought you could do with sweetening up."

I resisted the urge to stick my tongue out at him, but only barely. "So, why were you following me?"

Unfazed by my ungrateful attitude, he took a sip of his coffee and slouched back in his chair. The carefree posture was much more reminiscent of how he'd been when I'd first met him, and completely at odds with the expensive suit and business persona he was wearing now like an accessory.

"You mean, aside from keeping you out of trouble?"

"Funny. I'm pretty sure any trouble I've ended up in was thanks to your doing."

"Good times," he said with a wink.

My glare deepened, and the playfulness vanished from his face. Growing serious once more, he leaned forward and rested his elbows on the table.

"Do you know what those men would have done if they'd caught you?" he said, his voice low so that no one around us would hear.

"Sacrifice me?"

If my comment caught him by surprise, he didn't show it. Then again, I'd learned from harsh experience that Bres was the ultimate actor, so I couldn't trust any of his reactions to be genuine.

"They're dangerous men, Aisling. I'm trying to look out for you here."

"It's a bit late for that now," I snapped. "What does the Order have to do with the sons of Carmen?"

His expression became instantly shuttered, and he leaned back in his chair once more. "You were at the same meeting I was. It's a simple business deal. Don't go looking for trouble where there is none."

"I'm not looking for anything other than to be left alone. But any time I try that, you show up like a bad smell. So, come on, tell me. Are they picking the victims, or is the Order doing it? Let's face it, you both have plenty of motive for wanting the Watchers dead.

Though I have to admit, I didn't think even you'd stoop to something as horrific as this."

"I don't know what you're talking about."

"Sure you don't. So, the Order of the Fomori simply has legitimate business interests with the sons of Carmen?"

"The Order has a lot of legitimate business interests."

"And illegitimate, I'm sure."

He gave me a crooked grin, but the hard edge remained in his eyes. "It's good to keep life interesting."

Draining the end of his coffee, he placed the cup down on the table and stood. "I'll let you enjoy the rest of your lunch in peace. But trust me, Aisling, you don't want to keep sticking your nose in this. It won't end well."

I strongly considered not going back to the office after lunch. It was getting harder and harder to turn a blind eye to the fact the firm had zero morals as to who they worked with. I might not have been the one choosing the clients, but was I any better if I just stood by and said nothing?

Of course, moral high ground is all well and good, but it doesn't pay for things like food and rent – you know, living. So, feeling icky about my life choices, I went back and tried to keep busy so that the afternoon would pass with as little time for thinking as possible.

Concern for Pete still plagued me, so when work was finally finished and I was making my way to meet Brian, I tried to call him. It went straight to voicemail, and an ache settled in my chest as Pete's carefree voice instructed me to leave a message.

That was the Pete I remembered, not the tormented person who'd sat across from me in the café and confessed his fear of hurting someone. That was how he'd still be now if it wasn't for me.

The sombre thought refused to leave me as I made my way to the Fuzzy Duck, a popular after-work pub close to the financial sector of the city centre. Dimly lit with exposed stonework, the pub somehow managed to find the perfect balance between cosy privacy and vibrant socialising.

Brian was already waiting for me when I arrived. He'd chosen a table in one of the small nooks towards the back of the pub, away from the bustle of the bar. He seemed oblivious to my approach as he stared, lost in thought, at the pint of Guinness in front of him. Unease settled over me as I took in the dark circles under his eyes and the almost defeated slump to his broad shoulders.

"You look like shit," I said by way of greeting as I pulled out the chair across from him.

He jerked his head up in surprise and grimaced. Instead of offering a witty response, he waited until a young waitress came and took my drink order before speaking.

"There's been another murder."

I sucked in a breath.

"Last night in the Phoenix Park." He scrubbed a hand over his face, and I noticed the stubble coating his chin had grown significantly more pronounced since I'd last seen him. "The body was ... brutalised before the sacrifice, but the general details were the same."

It took a moment for what he was saying to sink in, but when it did, my blood ran cold. The Phoenix Park? Did it have anything to do with my attack? Was I meant to have been the fifth victim?

Brian straightened up, seeming to compose himself even as my own turmoil threatened to choke me. "You said in your message that you have information."

I nodded, feeling somewhat numb with the realisation of my narrow miss. "What do you know about the sons of Carmen?"

He frowned, concentrating. "Three sons and their mother. Came to Ireland, were defeated by the Tuatha and sent packing."

"Well, they're back. And I think I know who they are."

All signs of exhaustion disappeared from him so quickly that I flinched, wondering if I had imagined it. The look he fixed on me now was sharp and alert, the keen watchfulness making it clear that I would be hard-pressed to get anything past him.

"Tell me," he ordered.

Though I'd already told him about the strange man I'd seen in St. Stephen's Green park, and his subsequent attack on me in the Phoenix Park, I started at the beginning. As I reminded him of the two incidents, it was clear he'd already come to the same realisation I had – we both knew it was little more than luck that allowed me to be sitting here now.

Swallowing to clear my suddenly dry throat, I told him about my suspicions that the sons of Carmen were working with the Order. I made a point of stressing that I had no proof Dothur was involved with any of this, but the argument sounded lame, even to my own ears.

Brian listened carefully the whole time, interrupting only when he required further clarification. At no point did he sit back and laugh at my overactive imagination, and I understood with pained resignation that I'd been right to trust my gut. Though I didn't want to believe myself to yet again be a terrible judge of character, I wasn't going to ignore the warning signs. Not this time.

"Can you get me the address for Carmen Holdings?" he asked when I was finished speaking.

Years of conditioning caused an uneasy feeling to settle over me at the thought of breaking client confidentiality. But I'd done it before to find the Order of the Fomori when Bres was missing and I'd wanted their help. This time, people were dying.

"I'll get it for you in the morning, though I don't know if the premises is occupied. Will you pass it onto the police?"

It was a strange question to ask considering I was speaking to a Garda, and murder fell pretty clearly into law-breaking territory. But something told me that the police might not be equipped to deal with the sons of Carmen, even if magic was, as yet, impeded.

Apparently, Brian had come to the same conclusion.

"The Watchers will deal with it. It's best if the police keep their attention on the satanic cult angle for the moment."

We lapsed into silence, both lost in our own thoughts. I had no love for the Watcher who sat across from me, but for once it felt like we were at least in the same corner. Whether that would remain true by the end of this, I wasn't sure. Only time would tell.

CHAPTER SEVENTEEN

Exhaustion was dragging me down like a heavy weight by the time I got back to the apartment. The adrenaline that had been buzzing through my system ever since the meeting that morning had faded, and it felt like I could sleep for a week.

Of course, sleep wouldn't be restful for me tonight. I needed now more than ever to up my training. Maybe I'd be able to get the address for Brian and it would be enough for the Watchers to put an end to this whole sorry mess, but it still seemed like there was a noose around my neck waiting to tighten at any moment. I'd had a lucky escape in the park yesterday. I wasn't so sure I'd be as lucky next time.

A glance at my phone as the lift ascended the three floors told me Pete hadn't called or responded to any of my messages. I tried not to let the seed of concern implant too deeply; he had a lot to work through. It made sense that he'd need some time.

The hallway was dark when I stepped out of the lift. My chest tightened as I looked towards the door, the tension easing only when I confirmed there were no strange gifts waiting for me. Part of me had expected to see a dead bunny or something equally disturbing, which spoke volumes about how fucked up my life had gotten.

Wearily, I unlocked the door. I wanted nothing more than to fall into bed, but Teagan would be home from work shortly, and I couldn't put off talking to her any longer. As much as I tried to convince myself that one more night wouldn't make a difference, I knew deep down that she deserved to know the truth about what was happening to her.

I reached out to switch on the lights as the door clicked closed behind me, already dreading the conversation that was to come. A figure stepped out of the shadows that coated the kitchen, and I froze.

A warning shake of his head cut off my scream before it could emerge, and the magic that should have been my natural defence was nowhere to be found in the face of my sudden terror.

My assailant from the park wore the same leather jacket as before, and the shadows that shrouded him undulated as he moved. Piercing eyes were once again the only distinguishable feature on his face, but the mesmerising thrall they held was dulled significantly by the newfound understanding that I was staring into the eyes of a killer.

Casually, he pulled out a chair at the kitchen table and motioned for me to sit.

An overwhelming sense of panic threatened to drown me from within. I willed myself to turn and run, but somehow I knew I'd have no chance of making it out the door and to safety before he caught me. I was trapped.

When he gestured again to the table, I found my feet moving to do as he bid, his shadows winding their way around my legs. Breathing shallowly, I kept my eyes fixed on him for any sign of a threat as I pulled out the chair furthest away from him.

If he was insulted that I didn't accept the chair he'd offered, he didn't show it. Instead, his attention shifted to the rose that sat in the vase at the centre of the table. He reached a hand out and caressed the silky petals reverentially.

"Did you like my gift? When you left it in the box, I wasn't sure."

My mouth went dry. How did he know I'd left it in the box?

A terrifying realisation struck me. "You put it in the vase," I whispered.

He inclined his head, the shadows dancing around him as he did. "I wanted to give you a token of my affection so you'd know I was with you. When I saw it, I knew it was perfect." He prowled towards me and my breath hitched.

"Just like you," he said, running his fingers across my cheek in a featherlight touch.

I clenched my sweaty hands into fists to stop from flinching away. If I just played along, it would buy me some time. The magic was there somewhere; it had to be. I just needed to concentrate.

I swallowed once, then twice. "How did you get into the apartment?"

Through the darkness that swirled around him, I could've sworn I saw his lips curve up.

"There are shadows everywhere."

Well, fuck. It was a pretty safe bet that I was never sleeping again – assuming I got out of this alive.

"I wanted to see you." His body tensed, the shadows seeming to grow more agitated in their movements. "After the wolf interrupted us in the park…"

Every instinct I had screamed a warning at his shift in demeanour. I could barely keep the tremor from my voice as I fought through the paralysing fear to speak.

"I'm sorry about that. He was just trying to protect me."

The man took a step back, tilting his head in what appeared to be confusion. "Why would it need to protect you? I would never hurt you. You're the only one who understands me. I would never hurt you," he repeated, his voice rising in anger.

"I can see that now," I croaked out, hurriedly trying to calm him. "It's just with the murders and everything, it's been a scary time."

He grew deadly still, and I suddenly realised I'd made a mistake.

"Why would you need to worry about the

murders?" he asked, an unspoken warning in his silky-smooth tone.

This time it took a few attempts at swallowing before I could formulate an answer, and try as I might, there was no keeping the tremble from my voice.

"I wouldn't. I mean, I've heard about them on the news and the police haven't caught the killer, so it probably wasn't too smart for me to be out walking alone like that. I was lucky you came along when you did."

The shadows around him returned to their leisurely movements, and I sucked in some much-needed oxygen. Desperately I reached inside, seeking the spark of power that had been a constant low-level buzz at my core ever since I'd first accessed the magic. It was there but muted, just barely out of my reach.

The clock on the wall caught my attention and my stomach plummeted, my focus on the magic immediately lost. Teagan was due home any minute. I couldn't drag her into this. I had to do something.

Clambering for something, anything, that would get him out of the apartment before she returned, I blurted, "We should go somewhere."

I cringed inwardly at the high-pitched panic in my tone but pressed on. "I haven't had dinner yet. If you give me a minute to change –"

A firm hand on my shoulder halted me as I made to stand. "I'm not ready to share you with them just yet."

I fell back into the chair with a thud. Not sure I wanted to know the answer, I croaked, "With who?"

He continued, almost as if he hadn't heard the

question. "They don't understand. They don't appreciate how special what we have is."

His hand moved from my shoulder to cup my cheek. The panic that I was barely holding inside rose to suffocating levels. I swallowed it back, forcing myself to place my hand over his.

"We can show them. We don't have to hide in here like we're ashamed. It shouldn't matter that I'm the Guardian. If you can see past it, then –"

He reared back as if I'd struck him. The shadows that had calmed only moments before whirled and became a pitch-black eddy of fury.

"What did you just say?"

"I – I said we don't have to be ashamed," I stammered, knocking over the chair in my haste to stand and put distance between myself and the roiling mass of fury in front of me.

"You're one of *them*." He spat the last word, and the vehemence in his voice made the light bulb finally click on above my head.

He hadn't known who I was. He hadn't known that I was the Guardian, that I was descended from the very people who had banished him and imprisoned his mother. I'd just assumed he did, because he seemed to know everything about me.

A terrifying cold radiated from him as he whispered, "You lied to me."

"No. No, I didn't. I swear." I held up my hands as if that might stave off the attack that was sure to come.

Just then, a key jangled in the door. I had only a

second to realise I'd once again failed to keep my friend safe before the door swung open.

"Honey, I'm –" Teagan froze, taking in the scene before her. She screamed.

The sound pierced me to the core of my very soul, and something inside me shattered. The world went black.

CHAPTER EIGHTEEN

"Aisling? Oh god, Aisling, can you hear me? ... Hello. Yes, I need an ambulance, please..."

The words drifted through the darkness to me, piercing the fog that clouded my head. With a difficulty that belied thirty years of automatically firing synapses, I sent a message to my body to squeeze the warm hand that was holding mine.

I blinked my eyes open, only to be met with a searing pain in my head as the light pierced my retinas. Teagan's tear-stained face appeared in front of me, her eyes wide.

Dropping the phone she'd been holding to her ear, she grasped my shoulders and bent down until she was mere inches from me. Her eyes scanned every inch of my face as if to reassure herself she wasn't imagining my newly conscious state.

"You're awake. Oh thank god." Her voice cracked. "I thought you were..."

A hiss of static came from the phone on the ground beside me. "Miss ... Miss ... Are you still there?"

Teagan stared at the phone in surprise, clearly having forgotten about it in her concern for me. She moved to pick it up, but I grasped her hand.

"I'm fine. No ambulance."

Why did my voice sound so strange? And what the hell was I doing on the floor?

She looked like she wanted to argue, but I shook my head, biting back the groan that threatened as a jolt of pain made me see stars.

Reluctantly, she hung up the phone and helped me up to sitting. I could tell by the tight line of her mouth that she'd be pressing *redial* the instant I showed any sign of not being okay.

I ignored the pressure in my head and tried to focus as the room spun. The front door stood open, the side table that normally rested by the wall now lying on its side on the ground. The apartment was empty except for me and Teagan.

Panic tightened my chest as I searched frantically for the man in shadows. "What happened? Where is he?"

"It's okay, it's okay. He's gone," she assured me. Her tone was calm, soothing, but I could hear the tremble beneath it.

I furrowed my brow in confusion. "He just left?"

Surely he hadn't just excused himself and left? I'd had no doubt that he'd kill Teagan if she arrived home when he was still there. So, what stopped him?

My friend sat back on her heels, the sudden uncertainty in her expression creating an air of vulnerability that I wasn't used to seeing in her. I watched with concern as she worried at her lip.

"I don't know what happened. I came in and saw you surrounded by all these shadows. All I remember is screaming. Then everything went black. When it cleared, he was gone and you were lying on the ground." Her eyes glistened as she fixed me with a beseeching gaze. "Who was that man, Aisling? What did he want?"

I rubbed a hand over my face and was surprised to find red smeared on my hand when I looked down. Was that blood?

"Here." Teagan gently dabbed at my nose with a tissue she held crumpled in her hand.

As she did, I became aware of a dampness by my right ear. I poked at it and my fingertips came away red too. *Shit.* I looked from the blood to Teagan, and she grimaced.

"Your nose has been bleeding, and there was a small trickle from your ear. That's why I wanted to call an ambulance." She glanced at her phone as if still considering it. "I don't know if you hit your head when you collapsed or if that man hurt you. What the hell is going on?"

I motioned for her to help me up; my arse was going numb sitting on the ground. With her supporting me, I made it to the sofa and collapsed onto the cushions. She handed me a fresh tissue, but the bleeding seemed to have stopped when I dabbed at my nose.

"You know the sacrifices Siobhán came here about?"

Her eyes widened, but she nodded silently.

"I think he's the person responsible. Or one of them, at least."

Teagan turned ashen.

Guilt pressed heavily down on me as I realised just how much trouble I'd brought to her doorstep. This was Teagan's home. She'd generously welcomed me in when I had nowhere else to go, and this was how I repaid her. I wanted to hang my head, but I forced myself to face her and any recriminations that would come.

"I'm sorry, I –"

She held up a hand to stop me. "Tell me everything."

With a deep breath, I filled her in. I told her about the strange man at Siobhán's crime scene, how he'd later attacked me at the park, and how I'd returned home to find him here this evening. I explained Killian's theory about the sons of Carmen, and how, once again, it looked like the Order might be involved. The only thing I omitted was Pete's role in saving me, since that would've required me to explain about his wolf, and that wasn't my secret to share.

By the end, she was gaping at me with a horrified expression on her face. "And you think Dothur is involved in all of this?"

I sighed, once more marvelling at what a horrendous judge of character I was turning out to be. "I can't see how he wouldn't be. Even if he knows nothing about it, his brothers are clearly involved. If what Killian said is true, it's unlikely he's the only one of the three not here looking for some form of vengeance."

Teagan's eyes flicked to the rose that sat innocuously in the vase on the table, and she shivered. "God, that thing is so creepy now. I saw it this morning after you'd left for work and I assumed Dothur had sent it. I thought it was romantic."

Yeah, well, it was safe to say I'd never look at a rose as being romantic again. I scanned the room, reminded that its sender had been here not once but twice. Even the smallest shadows suddenly seemed more ominous after his comment, and I had to resist the urge to switch on every single light in the apartment.

I pushed the thought away; it would do me no good to dwell on it. Turning my attention back to Teagan, I shored up my resolve.

"There's something else you need to know."

She raised an eyebrow in question.

"After Siobhán came here, she wrote me a letter. She implied in the letter that there was something wrong with you. Something magical. I brushed it off as her trying to manipulate me, but..." I shook my head. "She said the Watchers would help you figure it out, but only if I help them with the sacrifices first."

Teagan grew still, her expression giving nothing away as she listened. I cast my eyes away.

"Brian refused to tell me anything, even after I went to the crime scene with him, so I talked to Killian. I explained everything that had happened leading up to Siobhán's letter. He said –" I swallowed hard, digging my nails into the palms of my hands. "He thinks you might be a banshee."

Silence met my words, and it was only with extreme effort that I forced myself to look up and meet Teagan's anger.

My friend sat on the other end of the sofa with a hand covering her mouth and her shoulders shaking. For a terrifying moment, I thought she was crying. Then the dam burst and she started giggling hysterically.

"A banshee? He thinks I'm a frickin' banshee?" She bent double, clearly finding the idea riotous.

I gaped at her, wondering if I'd officially pushed her over the edge of sanity. Then realisation struck me – she thought it was a joke.

"Brian confirmed it," I said softly, feeling even worse as the laughter died in her throat.

Her expression grew serious as she searched my face. "What do you mean?"

"It's true, Teagan. You're a banshee."

"How did she take the news?" Killian leaned against the tree next to me, arms crossed.

Though he appeared relaxed, I didn't miss the

tension still present in his carefully restrained movements after I'd filled him in on the evening's events. He seemed frustrated at not being able to do more to help, but when I'd pressed, he simply changed the subject to Teagan.

I sighed and hung my head. The crumbling log beneath me wasn't the most luxurious of seats, but it seemed fitting that I should suffer its discomfort; it paired nicely with my guilt.

"I don't know. At first she thought it was a joke. Then when she realised I was serious, she just went really quiet. The only time she showed any sign of being angry was when I told her it was possible her student had been one of the victims."

It had been fun breaking that titbit of information to her. The unbridled fury that flashed in her eyes had been a little scary to see, though it was understandable.

She hadn't berated me for keeping the information from her, but there had been a shadow of uncertainty lurking behind her eyes ever since, as if she was wondering what other lies or omissions I'd made.

"And tomorrow?"

An uneasiness set my stomach on edge as I thought about what was to come. "The Watchers will send people to scout out the location when I send the address. Once they give the green light, we'll go in."

We. Because instead of being compassionate or concerned for my well-being when I'd called Brian to let him know about the Darkness's visit, he'd bluntly informed me I would be accompanying them on the raid the next day. No matter how much I tried to disillusion him of the notion, he was convinced that the abilities bestowed on me as the Guardian would end this.

And if that wasn't enough, Teagan had overheard my protests and declared in no uncertain terms that she was coming too.

"She won't listen to reason. She's adamant that she's coming. How the hell am I supposed to protect her?"

Killian raised his eyebrows. "Why is it your responsibility to protect her? From what you've told me, she was the one who saved you from the Darkness."

I gaped at him, waiting for that stoic expression to crack into a smile to show me he was joking. It didn't.

"She wouldn't even be involved in any of this mess if it wasn't for me."

He shrugged. "Maybe. But she is involved, and she has as much right as you to be there and see it through to its conclusion."

Was he for real? I'd nearly gotten her killed once already by attracting that psychopath to her home, and now he wanted me to bring her along while we went to face off against three brothers who were likely immortal magic users?

"I'd happily be anywhere else. Brian is the one insisting I be there. He's still under the impression that I'm some magical secret weapon and I've just been playing dumb this whole time." I snorted, wishing that was true.

I thought I caught a shadow of concern passing

over Killian's face, but he covered it just as quick, clapping his hands together.

"Let's get to work."

I stood up reluctantly and brushed crumbling bark from my trousers. Killian was right; time was running out and we needed to train. But the memory of facing the Darkness lingered with me. I'd felt the magic flare to life when Bres had caught me spying, only for it to splutter out straight away. When I'd gotten home to find the Darkness there, I'd been so paralysed by fear that I hadn't even managed that much. What hope did that give me?

Angry with myself, I pushed the thought away. Teagan was going on that raid, no matter what I said. Despite what Killian believed, it was up to me to keep her safe, so I would do everything in my power to make sure I was ready.

Now that I knew how to search for the thread of magic within me, it came easier. Killian's words wrapped around me, comforting and familiar, but they weren't necessary anymore because this time, to my utter surprise, the magic came to me in a blaze.

Every synapse fired to life within me. I could feel the energy that powered those synapses, and the potential it held. I could also feel my desperation.

Somewhere in a distant part of my mind, I was aware of Killian urging me to calm my breathing and relax my mind. I ignored him as I reached for the power that called to me. So much power. Strong and vibrant, and mine for the taking.

This would help me face the sons of Carmen. This was what I needed. It didn't have to be hopeless, not if I had this.

The moment my thoughts turned to the three brothers, the magic flared white hot inside me. It flooded every cell in my body, stealing my breath away in a barrage of power. Euphoria turned the world into a kaleidoscope of colour around me, and I was lost in the infinite possibilities. Energy crackled across my skin, waiting for me to mould and shape it. It was mine, it was deadly, and it was beautiful.

For a long moment I was lost in the sensations. Then, from one breath to the next, the colours dimmed. My head suddenly grew light and the world started spinning. I reached for more magic, but it wouldn't come.

An unexplainable exhaustion settled over me. I tried to inhale, but a crushing force pressed down on my chest. Panic constricted my throat and I mentally scrambled for a surface that was no longer in sight.

With each desperate attempt to breathe, my energy faded further until I no longer had the will to fight. A blissful oblivion beckoned me forward even as the energy swirled around me in a vortex that was now out of reach.

There was a sharp sting across my cheek, and I jolted back to awareness with a gasp.

I had a moment to blink in confusion, taking in Killian's panicked expression, before my legs gave way beneath me and I crumpled to the ground.

Killian was at my side instantly. He knelt down next to me and gently cradled my head as he helped me to a lying position. "Can you hear me?" he asked, pulling up one of my eyelids and then the other.

When he proceeded to turn my head from side to side and click his fingers in front of my face, I slapped his hand away feebly. "I'm fine. I'm fine."

That was odd – why did my voice sound slurred?

He rocked back on his heels and ran a hand through his hair, clenching it into a tight fist as he tried to compose himself.

"Dammit, Aisling. What have I told you? *Never* tap into your own life force."

I stared dumbly at him. My brain couldn't seem to process what he was saying or why he was so angry. I hadn't...

He nodded as understanding slowly dawned on me. "You accessed the magic inside you, not the magic that's around you. You let your emotions drive you, and it sucked you in. You could have died."

Oh.

With a trembling hand, I brushed sweat-slicked hair back from my face. This was a dream world. It wasn't real. Yet something about Killian's expression told me that the threat to my life had been very real.

"I didn't mean to," I whispered. "It just came to me so easily. I didn't realise it was a different source."

He blew out a long breath, seeming to let go of some of the tension he'd been holding. "You weren't concentrating. You were so distracted that you didn't pay attention to what your instincts were telling you. If you can't separate yourself from your emotions here in this place..."

The rest of his sentence hung in the air unspoken between us, and I knew in that moment that I was screwed.

CHAPTER NINETEEN

"You can still change your mind." I flicked my eyes to Teagan, who had been silent since she'd met me at Smith & Mercer.

Clifford had demanded my undivided attention all morning, and my anxiety levels had ratcheted higher and higher until I finally managed to escape his prying gaze long enough at lunchtime to get the address for Carmen Holdings.

I'd sent it to Brian, half hoping he'd have reconsidered and would tell me to sit this one out, but he hadn't. Instead, he ordered me to meet him at the Docklands in an hour to wait for the green light from the scout team he was sending ahead.

Needless to say, Clifford was none too pleased when I informed him of the emergency doctor's appointment that would require me to leave work for the afternoon. I avoided too many awkward questions by informing him it was "women's problems," and thankfully he was too much of a Neanderthal to pry any further. The promotion I'd been waiting forever for was quickly slipping further and further away, however.

"I'll make sure the Watchers stick to their word and help you once this is sorted," I tried again when no response was forthcoming.

She gave me a sideways look that clearly said to stop wasting my breath, and I sighed in defeat.

Brian hadn't been fazed when I broached the subject of Teagan coming along. I'd been counting on him to veto the idea, but he'd simply grunted in acknowledgement and proceeded to bring me up to speed with the plan.

His single-minded focus was worrying. I knew how important it was to him that we stop the sons of Carmen, especially after what happened to Siobhán. But shouldn't he at least consider the appropriateness of putting a civilian in danger? Maybe Teagan's banshee status stopped her from being a person in his mind, the same way my being the Guardian allowed him to inflict dead bodies on me? I didn't know, but I sure as shit wouldn't be relying on him to watch either of our backs.

When I spotted the Watcher waiting for us at the end of the street, I knew time had run out for me to change Teagan's mind. I wiped my sweaty palms against my trousers and straightened my shoulders in an attempt to look like I wasn't about to wet myself with fear.

Brian's eyes were focused and alert as he watched us approach, and I had the sense that he was like a coiled spring, ready to act at a moment's notice. He was dressed in black jeans and a navy sweatshirt, making it clear that he wasn't here in his capacity as a Garda. I had only a moment to wonder if what we were doing was strictly legal before we reached his side.

"Teagan, Brian. Brian, Teagan," I said by way of introduction.

"The banshee." Brian gave an acknowledging tilt of his head.

Teagan's smile was glowing, and anyone who didn't know her like I did would easily miss the strained edge to it. I didn't, though.

"So, how do we do this?" I asked.

Brian had told me the plan the night before, but my nerves were already getting the better of me. I didn't know how prepared the Watchers were for what we were about to do, but I definitely wasn't, and the repetition gave me something to focus on.

"We've had people watching the address for the past hour. They've confirmed there's movement visible from outside, and no one has left during that time. We haven't been able to get a view of the inside, so we'll have to work from the plans we have of the building. I'm expecting the green light to move in the next ten minutes."

I shifted uncomfortably from foot to foot. "Would it not be better to wait until it's dark?" Or better yet, until never.

He shook his head. "The address is for a business. If we wait too long, they'll likely leave the premises. The last thing we want is to take this fight out onto the street for civilians to get caught in the middle."

My mouth went dry. I didn't bother pointing out that he had two civilians standing right in front of him, but the irony wasn't lost on me.

From the corner of my eye, I noticed Teagan had grown tense. It was comforting to know I wasn't the only one feeling nervous. I hoped it would encourage her to be careful at least, though I'd have still preferred if she sat this out.

"What do you need us to do?" she asked, her voice quiet but unwavering.

Brian looked her over, the assessment thoughtful rather than leery. "A head's up if we're all going to die would be good. Other than that, stay out of the way and don't get yourself hurt."

His attention turned to me and his expression hardened. "You, on the other hand, will take the lead with me. If these guys have access to magic like we believe, it's time for you to start pulling your weight."

I bristled at his snide tone but kept my mouth shut.

Between the magic failing when I faced the Darkness and nearly draining myself dry during training, I was pretty certain I'd be a liability more than a help. There was no point saying any of that to Brian, however. For one, I wasn't ready to admit the existence of my magic to him so overtly. Secondly, he'd already shown time and again that he was a stubborn, pig-headed ass.

So, when Brian indicated it was time to go, we followed in silence.

The walk to the rendezvous point took less time than I'd have liked. Hell, a week long hike would still have been too short if I'd had my way.

The rest of the team were waiting for us in a disused warehouse two buildings down from our target location. Three men and two women, all wearing black and looking like they'd just stopped shy of going full-on ninja. Brian didn't bother to introduce us, and since I didn't feel inclined to make any more friends in the Watchers of Danu, I simply gave them a small nod of acknowledgement.

As I watched them discuss the entry plan in hushed tones, I couldn't help but wonder about their qualifications for being here. Magic had been gone from Ireland for longer than all our lifetimes combined, so I doubted any of them were adept magic users. But what about combat? Did the Watchers train their people in things like that?

I didn't have long to muse on it before Brian returned to my side, scowling.

"We have the green light to go. Stay by my side, and don't do anything stupid. Understand?"

I resisted the urge to salute, the hyperactive butterflies in my stomach dulling my natural instinct to be snarky. As one, we filed out of the warehouse and edged along the narrow walkway. With each step we took, my heart pounded harder in my chest. Could it break my ribs if it beat with enough force? *That would be one way to get out of this*, I thought with a vague sense of growing hysteria.

Many of the buildings in the area had been updated with glass fronts and stainless steel trimming in recent years. Carmen Holdings was not one of these. Instead, the building boasted a nondescript red brick façade that had been liberally covered in graffiti. A single metal door was the only entry point visible from the street, and the two top floor windows were so grimy I doubted they'd allow even a sliver of daylight through.

Considering the air of money that Dothur had always projected, the building seemed an odd fit for a business he was most likely associated with. An uneasy feeling twisted my insides as I took in the general sense of disuse that surrounded the place.

Brian veered down a narrow alley at the side of the building, and I followed, glancing nervously behind me. We stopped at a rusted fire door that had seen better days, and one of the other Watchers squeezed past me. He pulled a strange-looking tool from the black rucksack slung over his shoulder, then proceeded to work on the door in silence while we watched.

After what felt like forever but was probably only a couple of minutes, there was a low creak and the Watcher prised the door open, revealing a dark corridor beyond. Brian gave the signal and we moved single file into the building.

Utter silence greeted us.

My heart thundered, and I placed my hand on my chest, convinced that everyone must be able to hear it too. A small voice in my head pointed out that there was still time to turn around and run, but when I looked behind me and spotted Teagan pulling up the rear with one of the Watchers, I knew I wouldn't be doing that.

According to the plans the Watchers had acquired for the building, there was a large open-plan warehouse at the end of the corridor. Offices occupied the second floor, and it was there that the scout team had reported seeing movement. If the brothers were here, that was likely where we'd find them. I just hoped there wouldn't be a few fun surprises before we made it that far.

CHAPTER TWENTY

The warehouse was empty. Completely.

Though logically I knew the business was likely a front for whatever the sons were doing for the Order, I'd still expected there to be something to give the impression that their new energy technologies were real. A stack of solar panels, even?

I stayed dutifully by Brian's side as the rest of the team moved ahead to scour the ground floor, just to be certain. It didn't take them long to confirm that there was nothing of note, but rather than making me feel relieved, this just set me on edge even more.

Every muscle in my body was tense as we made our way to the metal staircase that led to the upper level. Try as I might to be silent, the metal creaked and groaned with each step I took. Brian glared at me and I glared back, though inside I winced with every misstep.

We paused at the top of the stairs, listening for any

sign of movement. Once again, we were met with only silence.

Doors lined either side of the corridor, but only the one at the furthest end had a weak beam of light visible through the crack at the bottom. With a series of hand gestures from Brian that could have been rock, paper, scissors for all they meant to me, the other Watchers each moved to stand by one of the doors.

Once everyone was in place, Brian indicated for me to follow him to the final door, the one showing the light. My feet were glued to the spot, and it took an immense effort of will to make them move.

My heart hammered in my chest, the beat so violent I was certain it was going to explode. I forced myself to take slow, deep breaths and, half afraid to do it, half afraid not to, I reached down to that place at my core where the magic resided. I centred myself and sent my awareness outward to seek the energy around me. The magic came.

It was significantly weaker than it had been in the dreamscape, a mere trickle compared to the tidal wave that had almost drowned me. The tightness in my shoulders lessened as I tasted the magic and breathed a sigh of relief. It wasn't my own energy I'd drawn upon this time; it was the energy around me.

Brian pulled out a baton and my concentration faltered. Panic surged through me as he reached for the door handle, causing the magic to spike and then falter.

The door swung open. Nothing happened.

Fluorescent light spilled from the room, and I blinked against the sudden glare. A single wooden desk sat by the window, and dust mites floated in the air. It was empty except for a sheet of crisp white paper that rested on the desk.

I moved towards it, but before I had a chance to see what was on the page, Brian pushed past me and picked up. He growled, slammed it back down on the desk, and stormed out.

"Check the other rooms," he barked.

Curious as to what had caused the reaction, I picked up the paper with a trembling hand. Five simple words were written in elegant handwriting across the centre of the page.

Five down. Two to go.

An icy chill settled over me. They'd known we were coming. How? Had something tipped them off? Had the scouts been spotted?

My phone buzzed in my pocket, and I leapt out of my skin. Fuck, I hadn't remembered to turn it off; I could have given away our approach. *What a fucking idiot.*

Berating myself for my stupidity, I glanced down at the screen. The breath stalled in my chest.

How about that date I promised?

Dothur's name mocked me as I stared at my phone incredulously. Surely this had to be a joke.

Before I could think to alert Brian or the others to

what was going on, my phone buzzed again. This time a picture flashed up on the screen, and time fractured.

A wolf. Bound in silver chains.

I'd only seen Pete's wolf that one time in the Phoenix Park, but I knew without a doubt that it was him. The dark brown fur was the same colour as Pete's hair, and besides, it wasn't like there were many other wolves roaming around the place.

Another message buzzed through, and I almost dropped the phone in fright.

Church of the Blessed Heart. Come alone.

The "or else" was implied, but I had no doubt in my mind that Dothur would kill Pete if I didn't do as he said. I had no choice; I had to go back to the place where it had all begun.

The confirmation that the man I'd been dating had, in fact, been involved in this whole mess left me numb. Sure, it had been a pretty logical assumption, but to see the proof of it...

"They're not here. They must have cleared out before we arrived."

Brian's sudden return caused me to yelp. He scowled at me and at the white sheet of paper still gripped in my hand. "There must be another way out if the scout team didn't spot them leaving. Either way, we're back to square one."

My eyes darted to the darkness of the corridor

behind him. *Another way out, or lots of shadows to move between.*

I shivered.

"Maybe there's another address," I suggested, my mind working at a million miles an hour. "I'll go to the office. I'll check again." My voice sounded unnaturally high-pitched to my ears, and I cringed.

Brian eyed me with suspicion, but before he could question why I hadn't checked before – I had – one of the other Watchers called him to come look at something. I used the temporary distraction to slip past him into the corridor and hurried to the metal stairs.

Teagan stood at the bottom, looking around nervously as the others continued to search the building on the off chance there was something to find. Somehow I knew they wouldn't find anything that the sons of Carmen didn't want them to find.

"Guess it was never going to be that simple," she said softly as I approached.

Guilt gnawed at me. With the raid being a bust, there was no way the Watchers would give her the answers she needed any time soon. And with what I was about to do, they might not give them to her at all.

But Pete's life was on the line. I had no choice.

If by some miracle I survived the next few hours, I'd find a way to help her, no matter what it cost. For now, I had to make sure my ex-boyfriend didn't follow the wolves of Ireland into extinction.

"I'm going to head back to the office, see if I can find

another address for any of the brothers," I said, the lie sitting like ash on my tongue.

She moved as if to come with me and I quickly shook my head. "No. You stay with the others. I'll be right back. It'll look strange if I bring someone into the office with me after telling Clifford I had a doctor's appointment."

I didn't give her a chance to argue before I turned and hurried for the exit, but I felt her eyes follow me every step of the way.

CHAPTER TWENTY-ONE

It didn't take me long to hail a taxi once I got far enough from the warehouse to be seen. I blurted out the address and sat back to fidget anxiously as the driver navigated his way out of the city.

Only once I was sure I wouldn't be stopped did I respond to Dothur's message. Five simple words that would very possibly seal my fate: *I'm coming. Don't hurt him.*

It was early evening as we left Dublin behind. The still bright sun seemed to mock me with every mile we grew closer to the Church of the Blessed Heart – the place where, so many millennia ago, the Tuatha had sacrificed the strongest of their line. I hadn't been back there since my epic fuck-up on the solstice, but it seemed fitting to be going back now. I just hoped it wasn't my turn to make the ultimate sacrifice.

The city turned to motorway, and eventually to

rolling green hills. My head spun as I tried desperately to think of a plan.

Maybe I could bargain with them?

Of course, I wasn't sure what I had to offer that would make them give up a lifelong vendetta, so that possibility was probably slim enough as to be non-existent. Still, I clambered for any option that would get both Pete and myself out of this alive.

The roads narrowed considerably until there was barely enough room for a single car. Treacherous ditches bordered us on either side, and unconsciously I reached up and grabbed the "oh shit" handle.

My mind helpfully replayed the memory of Bres's car flipping and sending us careening into one such ditch during the car chase he'd staged. As I had many times since then, I mentally cursed him – and myself for falling for his lies.

Far too soon, the taxi pulled to a stop in one of the narrow lay-bys that lined the country road at the Church of the Blessed Heart. My stomach dropped as I realised there were no other cars around. Dammit, where were the tourists? Yes, it was midweek and late evening, but surely there should have been someone around.

The driver gave me a quizzical look and asked uncertainly, "You sure this is where you want to be dropped?"

I pasted what I hoped was a reassuring smile onto my face and held out two fifty euro notes. *No!* the terrified voice in my head screamed. *Please don't leave me.*

Out loud, I simply said, "This is perfect. Thank you."

My hand shook as I opened the door and climbed out. The cool breeze that brushed my cheek sent a shiver through me, and the smell of freshly cut grass tickled my nose. Silence greeted me, but it wasn't the usual calm of the countryside; there was nothing peaceful about this silence. It seemed unnatural somehow. As if nature itself was hiding its eyes from what was to come.

I wanted so badly to get back in the car and put as much distance between myself and this place as possible. Instead, I watched the taxi drive off, leaving me alone.

With effort, I forced my feet to carry me past the two large oak trees that framed the entrance to the old church grounds. By this stage, the sun had begun its descent towards the horizon and the evening was cast in crimson, adding further to the heavy sense of foreboding.

Aging headstones cast eerie shadows that jumped out at me as I walked. A rustle of leaves from the nearby trees sent my heart pitter-pattering in my chest. Everything that had made the place beautiful and intriguing to me on my first visit now felt sinister.

My destination wasn't the church grounds, rather the field that lay beyond them. From a distance, it looked completely innocuous compared to the ominous silhouette of the church ruins and the jagged edges of tombstones. But I knew what lay hidden in that seemingly empty field.

A cold sweat broke out along my spine that had nothing to do with the cooling of the evening. It felt like I had a giant target painted on me as I wound my way through the graveyard, the grass crunching beneath my feet. As I reached the remains of the old stone church, I edged along the wall, hoping the shadows it cast would help conceal my approach somewhat. A wishful dream.

The boundary wall came into view, and I spotted three men in the unnaturally perfect green field beyond. Dark shapes rested at the feet of two of them, but I was still too far away to make out what they were. My heart raced.

"You made it," Dothur called, his voice carrying easily on the light breeze.

I froze like a deer in headlights.

"Don't keep us waiting, now."

The two men standing at either end of the trio bent and lifted the bundles at their feet. I surged forward as I recognised Pete and his wolf.

"I'm here. I'm here. Don't hurt him."

I hurried to the wall and clambered over with all the finesse of a newborn foal. The three men followed my every movement with unnerving watchfulness as I hesitantly made my way closer to them.

Dothur stood at the centre of the trio with Dain on his left, and the man in shadows, who I knew only as the Darkness, on his right. With the three brothers standing next to each other, it was almost impossible not to see the resemblance. Even with the shadows swirling around the Darkness, it was clear that he bore the same tanned complexion and dark features of the other two. I kicked myself once again for being so goddamned oblivious.

My eyes darted to Pete. He hung limply from Dain's grip, and I could see no obvious signs of injury. I prayed to god he was merely unconscious.

His wolf was wrapped in silver chains, just like it had been in the photo Dothur sent. The Darkness held it roughly by the scruff of the neck, and my heart clenched in fear for the animal.

What would happen to Pete if the wolf was killed? Would he survive?

When I finally turned my attention back to Dothur, no trace remained of the man I'd shared dinner with. The eyes that met mine were dark and soulless, the mask clearly removed.

"So good of you to join us. I believe you've already met my brothers, Dain and Dub."

I swallowed hard and, determined not to let him see how scared I was, I straightened up. "I did as you said. Now, let him go."

"Not just yet."

I opened my mouth to protest, but he cut me off with a chilling look.

"First, you're going to help us cross the illusion spell."

"What?" I stammered. "I don't know what you're talking about."

"Now, let's not play coy. I'd hate for one of my brothers to accidentally hurt your friend here."

Panicking, I held up my hands to stop him before he could order them to do so. "I swear. I don't know how to get you across. I haven't got any of the soil."

The first time I'd unknowingly crossed the illusion spell that kept the Tuatha Dé Danann's ritual site hidden, I'd suffered a fun seizure. It was only when Bres had given me some of the soil from within the ritual circle that I'd been able to pass through unhurt. I'd thrown that soil away after the solstice, vowing never to return to this place again. Ha, talk about wishful thinking.

Dothur shook his head, tutting. "My dear Aisling. You really are clueless, aren't you? Your magic is tied to the spell. Now that magic has returned, you can cross freely anytime you wish."

Oh, shit.

He indicated to the slightly raised area of grass behind him with a wave of his hand. "So, if you'd please lead the way."

I hesitated. Whatever they wanted to gain access to the stone circle for wouldn't be good, but I highly doubted their intentions would be any more pure standing around here either.

As if to prove my point, Dub shook the wolf held in his grasp. The silver chains jangled and there was a low, pained whine that caused my stomach to flip.

"Okay," I blurted. "I'll do it. Just don't hurt him."

Dothur stepped aside to clear a path for me to pass, his cold expression unwavering.

I moved forward, my breaths growing more strained the closer I got to the brothers. By the time I drew level with Dothur, I was all but hyperventilating. He placed a hand on my shoulder and I'd have screamed if my vocal cords hadn't seized up in terror. His grip was like steel pressing down on me, and there was a knowing glint in his eyes.

"Contact is required for us to come with you," he clarified.

Another hand clamped down on the opposite shoulder, and I jerked my head around to find myself face to face with Dain's angry glare. Rage emanated from him in waves, and I had the sense that I was one wrong breath away from violence. I looked away quickly.

Dub thankfully didn't reach out to touch me but clasped Dothur's shoulder, the connected contact apparently enough.

Dothur nudged me forward and the shimmery boundary of the illusion spell appeared before me. I closed my eyes, terrified to take the final steps in case he was wrong about needing the soil.

Electricity skittered over my skin and the air shifted. With a shaky breath, I opened one eye and then the other. No longer was I standing in an empty field. Instead, I found myself between two large standing stones. Five other stones completed the circle, each with a jagged crack running down their centre. The earth beneath my feet was blackened, and the few remaining patches of grass within the circle were parched and brittle.

"This will do nicely." Dothur released his hold on my shoulder and strode into the centre of the circle, a flask in his hand that I hadn't noticed previously.

I took a shuddery breath, apprehension quickly overshadowing my relief at making it across safely. "For what?"

He turned those soulless eyes on me and smiled. "For the final sacrifices, of course."

CHAPTER TWENTY-TWO

"You can't do this," I pleaded as Dain and Dub tied Pete and his wolf to two adjacent standing stones. "You said you'd let him go if I came alone."

Dothur stopped and seemed to consider this. "Did I? I believe I simply said to come alone. I never said he'd live if you did."

My heart stopped. Oh god, he was right. At some point I'd convinced myself that they'd let Pete go if I just played along with their game, that I wasn't just unnecessarily sacrificing myself. But that wasn't what Dothur's message had said.

"He's no use to you for the sacrifice. He's not Tuatha. Let him go." Desperation tinged my tone, but I no longer cared about putting on a brave face.

At the mention of the Tuatha, a low snarl came from Dub and the shadows around him grew agitated.

Dothur glanced at him but appeared unsurprised by the reaction. "Fair point," he conceded, returning his attention to me as he opened the flask he held in his hand.

For a split second, relief loosened the tightness in my chest. Then I saw the gleam of satisfaction in those black eyes, and my blood ran cold.

"Of course, it's not actually necessary for the sacrifices to come from the Tuatha Dé Danann lineage. That was simply a bonus for us, but any death will do to generate the energy. And a werewolf's magic is particularly potent. It's perfect for our goal."

I struggled to swallow as my churning stomach pushed bile up my throat. "What goal is that?"

"Nothing you need to concern yourself with," Dub snapped, his shadows calming around him in a manner that scared me even more than their agitation had.

Dothur gave him a warning look. "Suffice it to say, our mother will be avenged. Whether by our hand or her own."

Her own hand? But their mother was dead.

Confused, but knowing I needed to keep them talking to buy myself more time, I pressed, "I understand why you blame the Tuatha for what happened to your mother, but the people you're hurting now had nothing to do with it. They're innocent."

"You understand?" Dain roared, punching the standing stone he'd just strapped Pete to.

I flinched back, having completely forgotten about the third brother as I tried to reason with Dothur.

"You understand nothing, little girl," he snarled.

Dothur held up a hand. "Enough," he commanded, casting his eyes up to the crimson sky above us. "It's time to get started."

My heart thundered as a feeling of utter hopelessness threatened to choke me. Something sparked deep within my core, and I reached for it as a drowning man would a lifebuoy. Magic – my only hope.

The power was stronger than it had been back at the warehouse. Whether that was because the distance from the city allowed for a better connection to nature and the magic of the land, or because the stone circle helped to augment it, I wasn't sure. But I was suddenly aware of the buzz of energy that surrounded me. It was there, ready to be used. If I could just figure out how.

As I wracked my brain to remember everything Killian had shown me the night before, Dothur walked in a wide circle, tipping over the flask he held. Red liquid flowed from it and splashed on the parched earth beneath his feet.

"Is that..." I swallowed.

Dothur raised an eyebrow. "Blood? Yes. Courtesy of the previous five sacrifices."

He didn't elaborate any further, but I didn't need him to tell me that the blood was generating power – I could feel it crackling in the air around me, seeming to suck all the oxygen from the space.

I clenched and unclenched my fists at my sides, my body caught between the need to act and the crippling paralysis of fear. Silently, I willed more magic to me from the earth, but it wasn't enough. It built at my centre, flowed through my veins, but I had no idea what to do with it.

Dothur joined the ends of the circle, and I knew my time was almost up. The air became charged, and with sickening realisation I understood exactly what natural energies the brothers had been cultivating for their business.

He turned to me. "Now, who wants to volunteer to go first?"

I opened my mouth to beg him to let Pete go, to just take me. I was the Guardian. Surely that had to count for something? The sound of a car in the distance caused me to snap my mouth shut.

Had someone found us? Could I attract enough attention to get help?

The sound grew closer and the three brothers stilled, each fixing their attention on the horizon. The engine cut off abruptly, and I heard a car door opening in the not too far distance.

This was it, the only distraction I would get. Even if someone had found us, they wouldn't be able to see us through the illusion veil. I couldn't just stand around here hoping for a saviour to arrive.

I made a last desperate attempt to pull as much magic to me as I could. My weight shifted as I marked the position of each of the brothers. Dothur was closest to me at the centre of the circle, with Dain and Dub on the far side next to Pete and his wolf. If I could take Dothur by surprise –

"Aisling?"

The magic I was holding within me spluttered and died, my heart freezing in my chest as I heard Teagan's call.

A slow smile spread on Dothur's face, and the look he gave me turned my blood to ice.

He gave the barest nod of his head and suddenly Dub was at my side, a bruising grip locked onto the back of my neck. Shadows caressed my cheeks and my lips as he whispered in my ear. "Shhh."

"Aisling. Are you out here?" Teagan called again, still out of sight but growing closer if the sound of her voice was any indication.

Helplessly, I willed her to turn around and leave. There was no need for Dub's warning because the last thing I wanted was to add my best friend to this fucked-up party.

But I had clearly pissed off the Fates at some point in my life because a couple of the longest minutes of my life later, Teagan came into view at the boundary wall that separated the church and field.

"No." I shook my head, whimpering. "Turn around. Please."

Even as I quietly begged, she climbed over the low stone wall. She stood there for a minute, scanning the field.

Teagan had been with me the first time I'd crossed the illusion spell and taken the seizure. She knew all about the ritual circle and what lay hidden from sight in this innocuous-seeming field. I had no idea if she'd be able to find it, though. Or what might happen to her if she did.

I opened my mouth to yell a warning to her, not willing to take any chances with her life when I'd likely already doomed myself and Pete. Shadows flooded my mouth, choking out any sound I might make, leaving me struggling for breath.

Through the tears that filled my eyes, I saw Teagan freeze. Her gaze fixed on the area where the ritual site lay and with steely determination, she strode forward.

I watched in horror as she grew closer, unable to act thanks to the shadows that had wrapped around me in binds so tight I could barely blink, let alone cry out to her.

Everything slowed to minute movements, and my mental screams grew louder and louder.

As she neared the edge of the illusion and reached out a hand, her eyes flashed purple. The shadows released me, and the scream tore free of my throat just as Teagan touched the veil.

CHAPTER TWENTY-THREE

I waited for the seizure to hit Teagan, for her to fall to the ground, struck by whatever protections had been built into the illusion spell to keep people away. She just stepped straight through.

Shock registered on her face as her eyes fell first on me, then on her surroundings. She froze and her skin turned ashen.

"Good to see you again." Dub's shadows released their hold on me and darted out towards her.

I screamed as they locked around Teagan's throat.

She clawed at the inky tendrils, eyes growing wide in panic. Her fingers passed straight through and the shadows constricted further, lifting her from the ground until her feet were flailing beneath her.

"Let her go," I cried.

I tried to run to her, but Dub wrapped a bruising grip around my arm and no matter how much I struggled, I couldn't break free of it.

"Enough," Dothur ordered, his voice sounding almost bored. "It's time to get started."

At his words, Dub released his grip on both me and Teagan, who fell to the ground with a wheezing gasp. The shadows remained loosely around her throat as Dub walked back to stand next to Dothur.

Dothur gave the barest nod of his head and Dain, who had watched with silent amusement, moved from his position next to Pete to loom over Teagan. Only when he was there did the shadows recede fully.

"Aisling, if you would do us the honours." Dothur indicated with a hand to the blood circle at his feet. "I had planned to keep you for the final sacrifice, but I think it would be best for you to lead by example."

I gaped at him incredulously. Was he fucking crazy? He expected me to just lie down and play dead for him?

"Come now. I'm sure you don't need us to explain why co-operation would be best."

Taking his cue, Dain grabbed Teagan by the hair and yanked her up from the ground. She bit back a cry of pain and glared at him, defiance blazing in her eyes.

I held up my hands in surrender, the thought of watching her be hurt more than I could bear. A sense of utter hopelessness overwhelmed me, and it was impossible to miss the satisfaction in Dothur's expression.

With nothing else to do, I attempted to again reach for the magic that had slipped through my grasp. I could feel it charging the very air I was breathing, could feel it skittering across my skin, but try as I might, I couldn't calm my rising panic enough to take hold of it. Fear gripped me tight and tears pricked the back of my eyes.

Dothur began chanting in a low voice, clearly satisfied that I would comply – one way or the other. Next to him, Dub closed his eyes and spread his arms out wide.

The shadows came at his call. They coalesced into a swirling vortex before him, and as Dothur's chanting grew louder, the vortex expanded until it filled the blood circle.

The hairs on the back of my neck stood on end as magic filled the space between the standing stones. It coated my tongue, leaving a vile, bitter taste in my mouth. It felt wrong, unnatural. As if the very magic was being tainted by Dothur's words.

His words grew faster and louder until he reached a crescendo. There was an almost inaudible *pop* – and everything went silent.

Nothing moved except for the shadows within the circle and the beat of my heart within my chest. It was as if time stood still.

When Dothur finally turned to me, there was an odd luminescence behind his gaze that made him appear even more terrifying. The air vibrated with energy, and every primal instinct within me screamed in warning.

He crooked a finger at me, and an inexplicable pull drew me forward.

I fought for all I was worth, digging my heels into the barren soil. Even so, the edge of the blood circle grew closer, and only sheer force of will stopped me from stumbling head first into the vortex of shadows within it.

From across the void, Dub's piercing gaze bore into me with a hatred that was almost tangible. He moved his hands, and strands of shadow shot out of the circle. They wrapped around my wrists and ankles like vices.

"No!" Teagan shouted. "Let her go."

The last word was accompanied by a sharp crack as Dain backhanded her across the cheek. Blood sprayed from her nose, and a strangely blank look settled over her features.

I had only a second to register the purple that once more flashed in her eyes before the shadowy manacles yanked me forward.

I fell to my knees, my hands landing in the blood-soaked earth. Power surged through me and my back bowed. Every nerve in my body lit up as I dug my fingers into the soil.

The taint was clear the moment I touched the magic. A blackness permeated the natural purity of the land, and the land rebelled against it. My head swam with the vileness of it, but still I pulled the magic to me.

The ground around me trembled, a light tremor at first, building to an undulation that rattled my bones.

"Aisling." Dothur's voice was a low warning.

I ignored him, focusing only on the magic.

Cracks formed in the earth, moving outward from

my hands. I ground my teeth together against the growing force of the power, and held on as if my life depended on it – because it most likely did.

"Is nobody going to stop this bitch?" Dain growled as the standing stone next to him shook.

He flung Teagan aside and in three large strides closed the space between us. His foot connected with my ribs with such force that my body lifted from the ground.

The crack of bone registered a split second before the pain hit.

My vision swam and I was pretty sure I screamed, but Teagan's terrifying shriek swallowed any noise I made.

The noise filled my head until it felt like my skull was going to split apart at the seams. I was made and unmade, all previous pain forgotten in the face of this beautifully agonising feeling.

I curled in on myself and covered my ears with my hands. Wetness coated them, and some part of me knew it was my lifeblood seeping from my body.

Dain was on his knees next to me. Through blurred vision, I could see the pain contorting his features as bloody tears streaked down his face. He let a furious roar and fixed his attention on Teagan, who was still screaming though she should have long ago gone hoarse.

Slowly, as if moving through sludge, he pushed to his feet, body bowing against the onslaught of the banshee scream. He took a step towards her, then another, murderous intent written in every clenched muscle and bulging tendon.

"No," I rasped.

I threw a hand out and caught hold of his ankle. He snarled and tried to shake me off, but I held on for all I was worth. I would not let him kill Teagan.

Every cell in my body felt like it was being shredded as I clung on, the pain sapping my energy at a terrifying speed. In sheer desperation, I reached out for the nearest source of magic.

A torrent of energy flooded through me. The pain that had all but consumed me was washed away in an instant. I gasped for breath as every part of me was filled with renewed life. Energy filled each atom, each molecule, and the world snapped into crystal-clear focus. I was floating, no longer tethered to something as insignificant as my human form. It was intoxicating, exhilarating, and I wanted more.

Then I saw him.

Dain lay on the ground next to me, his eyes staring lifelessly. My hand was still locked onto his ankle, and I yanked it away as if I'd been burned.

The flood of energy cut off immediately. And a sickening realisation struck me as I felt the sudden void where the source of power had been.

Had I done this? Had I somehow tapped into his life force? Oh god, had I killed him?

I covered my mouth to smother the scream that threatened to break free and push me over the edge of sanity for good. The energy still thrummed through me, and with every pulse of power, bile burned my throat.

The guilt was so crippling that it took me a moment to notice the silence. *Oh fuck, Teagan.*

Panicked, I twisted away from Dain's sightless eyes to seek out my friend.

I spotted her crumpled in a heap by one of the standing stones. Dothur loomed over her, blood running from his nose. He slashed the back of his hand across his nose to wipe it away, looked at his fallen brother. Then turned his attention to me.

CHAPTER TWENTY-FOUR

Dothur's hands were around my throat before I could scramble away. He hauled me to my feet and I clawed at his iron grip, fear consuming me as the flow of oxygen lessened and my head swam.

I expected to see rage in his black eyes, fury at what I'd done to his brother. But they were as cold and emotionless as they had been before, and that was even more terrifying than his anger could have been.

Between one non-breath and the next, I found myself back at the blood circle. Shadows no longer swirled within it, having receded to gather over a slumped form that I could only assume to be Dub. But the tainted energy remained, filling the circle like sludge that choked me as surely as Dothur's hands.

"You should have come alone," he said, flinging me to the ground. "Now your friends are going to die slowly and painfully."

I gasped for breath and sobbed, feeling broken and

defeated. I had come alone and it hadn't mattered. They'd never had any intention of letting Pete go. And now Teagan would die too.

Dothur began to chant once more, and the air grew heavy. It crushed me with its oppressive force and I couldn't move, no matter how hard I tried.

Though the earth beneath me was hard, it felt like I was sinking into it, being swallowed whole. I attempted to reach for the magic, but it choked me with its vileness.

Dothur dropped to his knees beside me and pulled a dagger out from under his jacket. The blade was as long as his forearm and wickedly sharp. Intricate symbols decorated the hilt, and they glowed and pulsed with his words.

"Be grateful I'm not going to make you witness their suffering before you die." He raised the dagger in the air. "As much as it would please me, your sacrifice is too important."

He plunged the blade down.

Sheer desperation to survive allowed me to break the paralysis that held me. I grabbed his arm, the dagger halting so close to my chest that I was terrified to breathe.

His strength was overwhelming, and I knew that, even with the benefit of Dain's life force flowing through me, I wouldn't be able to hold him for long. But I couldn't let him win, I just couldn't.

So, I did the one thing I knew I shouldn't do – I reached for my own life force.

Delving down deep inside myself, I locked onto the magic at my core. It was familiar and comforting, as if it had been there my entire life. I opened myself to it, embraced the desire to live, and prayed that I'd be able to stop in time.

The magic came in a deluge. It seared my soul as it flooded my veins, my muscles, my very being. Strength came where it had a moment ago been failing.

I drove Dothur's arm back up, affording me some much-needed breathing space. He snarled in response and met my increased strength with his own.

Sweat ran in rivulets down my forehead, and my arms trembled as I fought against him. My head was swimming from the power that filled me, but I knew it wouldn't last.

Killian had warned me how fine the line was before the very essence of life was drained, but I could see no other choice. I had to stop them, no matter the cost.

That line came much sooner than I expected, and I was hit with a sudden fatigue unlike anything I had ever felt before.

My vision faltered, and the blade dropped, piercing my sternum. Pain burned through me, followed by a strange peacefulness. It was fine. I just had to close my eyes and rest. Everything would be fine.

I blinked sluggishly as my mind struggled to remember why I was fighting so hard. What would be the harm in giving in?

Dothur leaned close to my cheek and took a deep inhale. "I do so love that smell of impending death.

There is something about that final spark of life that is just delicious."

Satisfaction glinted in his soulless eyes as he straightened back up, and a fierce defiance flared to life within me. Black crept in around the edges of my vision, and I knew I had crossed the line of no return. But if I was going, he was damn well coming with me.

With the last vestige of energy I had, I locked my hands around Dothur's wrists.

Something like surprise flashed across his face before realisation struck. He tried to jerk back out of my grasp, but I held on with the determination of a dying woman clinging to that last thread of life.

I focused my concentration outwards, letting go of the tenuous hold I still had on my own magic, and locking onto Dothur's. I called it to me.

The magic that came to me was poisonous. It was everything that was wrong and unnatural in the world. It was stolen energy borne of pain and death and suffering. But I took it. I allowed it to flow into me and I used it against him. And in the process, I allowed it to stain my very soul.

As I watched the life leach out of his eyes, there was a furious roar from nearby.

Dothur slumped forward as if to fall on me but was suddenly yanked backwards by thick tendrils of shadow. I had a moment to view the blood-red sky above me before there came an inhuman scream filled with grief.

A swirling vortex of shadows appeared around me,

lifting me from the ground. Too exhausted to fight any longer, I closed my eyes and welcomed the darkness.

"Aisling. Can you hear me?"

The words permeated the murky fog that clouded my mind, and I blinked in confusion. Blue eyes stared down at me only to drift out of focus again. Never-ending blackness swallowed me once more.

The world moved and my body was suddenly weightless. I was distantly aware that someone was carrying me, but my eyes were too heavy and didn't want to open.

"I told you to stay out of it," the voice said. "You just wouldn't listen, would you?"

It was so familiar. I knew the voice, but every time I tried to remember how I knew it, the exhaustion sucked me back under. I was floating in a timeless void, and though some part of my mind kept insisting it was important that I wake up, I couldn't bring myself to care. There was comfort in the darkness, and I wanted to stay cocooned in it forever.

A jostling sensation interrupted the blissful oblivion and I curled in on myself, not ready for the harsh light of reality to flood back in.

"They'll be here soon," the voice told me. "Don't die before then."

And then there was silence once more.

CHAPTER TWENTY-FIVE

"You're determined to make my job difficult, aren't you?"

Reluctantly, I turned my attention from the warm sun that bathed my face in its healing warmth and looked towards the copse of oak trees where Killian stood. A wry smile told me he was teasing, but the amusement didn't quite reach his eyes.

I wrapped my arms around my knees and pulled them in closer to my chest. "Am I dead?"

He choked out a surprised laugh and ran a hand through his messy brown. "Is this what you pictured the afterlife to look like?"

I considered the question as I scanned the bright, cheery meadow. The grass beneath me was soft and lush, the air always fresh and invigorating. Despite never seeing another person here aside from Killian, I'd always felt that the place was full of life, full of potential. It could be a kind of heaven, I supposed.

In that case, it probably wouldn't make sense for me to be dead – I wasn't going to heaven.

Tears pricked the back of my eyes. I rested my head on my knees and stared into the distance, unable to face him as I said, "I killed them."

"I know."

I swallowed, my throat constricting. "I can feel it inside me. The taint. I feel dirty, like there's a black smudge on my soul and if I even breathe wrong, it will grow bigger. Did I take part of them into me?" I looked at him finally, my desperation for reassurance outweighing my shame. "Am I evil now, too?"

He shook his head and pushed away from the tree to come sit next to me. His shoulder pressed against me, and after a moment's hesitation I leaned my head on it. When he didn't pull away, I allowed myself to relax into his warmth.

"You're not evil," he said, after what felt like an eternity. "But you have crossed a line. You've taken someone's life force. They would have killed you if you didn't, but that kind of magic, it leaves a mark."

An icy chill crept slowly through my veins. "What kind of mark?" I asked in a whisper.

"For some, the power proves to be addictive. For others, it twists their own magic into something unnatural. For you? I guess we'll see."

A blinding light seared through my eyelids, and I cringed away from it. The solace of darkness was gone, replaced only by pain. I peeled my eyes open and shut them again immediately as my senses were assaulted by the fluorescent light that glowed above my head.

"You're awake."

My eyes shot open at the sound of Teagan's voice and I found my friend standing over me, concern creasing a forehead that sported a large bandage on one side. A nasty purple bruise surrounded the eye beneath the bandage and her lip was cut and swollen.

Memories came flooding back in a tidal wave, and I bolted upright in wide-eyed panic.

Agony shot through my body, and for a moment, I was back in the blackness. Then it receded and Teagan was there by my side, a hand supporting my elbow.

"It's okay. Don't try to move. You're safe now."

I blinked and looked around in confusion. Where was I?

Generic cream walls surrounded me instead of the circle of standing stones. Though just as uncomfortable, the surface I was now lying on turned out to be a bed covered in crisp white sheets rather than the hard earth. And most importantly, I was surrounded by beeping machines and wires as opposed to a sacrificial circle of blood. A single window allowed me a glimpse of daylight beyond the room, but the view of the neighbouring brick building told me little of my location.

"Where are we?" The words came out hoarse and

sent a raw ache through my throat. I winced at the pain – and that, too, hurt.

"The headquarters of the Watchers of Danu." Teagan eyed me warily, as if afraid of my reaction. "They brought us back here after they found us at the church. Two nights ago."

Two nights ago?

I furrowed my brow, struggling to make sense of the puzzle. The last thing I remembered was the shadows waiting to consume me. Teagan had been unconscious, and Pete –

"Oh god. Pete!"

"It's okay. It's okay." Teagan held up her hands, hurrying to reassure me. "He's here too."

The knot of panic in my chest eased only marginally at her words. I needed to see for myself. I needed to be sure.

Looking unhappy but keeping her protests to herself, Teagan helped me out of bed. The tiled floor was cold beneath my feet, and I focused on that sensation rather than the aches and pains that were competing for attention in every part of my body. It took me a minute before my legs stopped shaking enough to hold my weight, but I stubbornly straightened as much as I could, determined to not to show weakness given our current location.

The corridor outside my room was empty and equally as nondescript as the room had been. There was a vague sterile smell that reminded me of a hospital, and I couldn't help but wonder why the Watchers would need a hospital wing in their headquarters.

As it turned out, we didn't have far to go before finding Pete. Teagan led me to a large glass window that showed a white room beyond. A single bed occupied the room with scary-looking machines surrounding it. Pete lay in the centre of the bed, his skin almost as pale as the sheets that covered him. He didn't appear to be awake, but I could see the rise and fall of his chest, and the stats on the monitor next to him appeared to be stable – at least to my untrained eye.

I swallowed hard as guilt constricted my throat.

There was no sign of the wolf in the room with Pete. Did that mean the creature had been reunited with him? Or did it mean something else?

"They've had to keep him in an induced coma while his body heals," Teagan said quietly. "They said the silver is poisonous to him, that it reacts with…" She trailed off with a sigh. "He's fighting it, but it caused him to spike a fever and they had difficulty controlling it because his body has been rejecting the medication. He came out the other side of it last night, and they're confident he'll live. The isolation is just a precaution."

Precaution from what? I wondered. To stop him from catching something? Or were they afraid that he'd pass something on?

I brushed that thought aside and focused on the positive – Pete was alive. I wasn't sure how to ask about his wolf, so for now, that would have to be enough.

"How did the Watchers find us?" I asked, turning to Teagan, suddenly confused. "I didn't think they were able to cross the illusion spell." At least Brian and Siobhán hadn't on the night of the solstice.

Teagan frowned. "They didn't have to cross it. When they got to the church, they found us all lying in the field next to the stone wall. I've no idea how we got there. I only regained consciousness shortly after they arrived."

It was my turn to frown at that. A vague memory flashed into my mind. Blue eyes. A familiar voice. Someone else had been there with us. Someone I knew.

Too weary to examine the thought in too much detail, I asked, "How did you find me, for that matter?"

She gave me a sheepish grin that did little to chase away the shadows in her eyes. "I used the Find My Friend app we set up on our phones after the solstice. I knew there was something off when you left the warehouse, so I followed you. I sent Brian the address when I got there and realised something wasn't right."

I knew I should be grateful, but fear tightened my chest as I remembered how close I'd come to losing her. How close we'd all come to dying.

I'd seen the portent in Teagan's eyes when they'd turned purple. Someone had always been destined to die in that place. It was only by some insane miracle of luck that it hadn't been us.

We lapsed into silence, each lost in our own

thoughts and the memories that would no doubt haunt us for a long time to come.

The sound of approaching footsteps caught me off guard and set my heart racing. It took me a moment to calm enough to recognise Brian's stocky frame and perpetual scowl as he approached us.

He gave me a curt nod in greeting – no "good to see you up, glad you didn't die" – before turning to Teagan. "You ready to start your training?"

She gave me an apologetic look. "Will you be all right on your own for a bit?"

I gave a vague nod, having the sense that I'd missed quite a bit in the time I spent unconscious. Now wasn't the time to ask, however. Not here.

As she moved to leave with Brian, I called after them. "Wait. How many bodies were there? Aside from us, I mean."

Brian gave me a strange look. "Two," he said, then turned and headed down the corridor with Teagan following on his heels.

I watched them go with an uneasy feeling. Only when they were out of sight did I cast my eyes around in search of shadows and shiver.

Aisling's troubles continue in The Guardian's Choice

GET YOUR COPY

https://books2read.com/theguardianschoice

NOTE FROM THE AUTHOR

Thank you for joining me on this adventure through Ireland's hidden (for now) supernatural world. This is entirely a work of fiction, so while I have taken inspiration from well known Celtic myths, I hope you'll allow me some poetic license with these as I build this new and exciting world.

If you enjoyed this book, I would be very grateful if you could leave a brief review (it can be as short as you like) on the site where you purchased your copy.

As an author, reviews are the most powerful tools in my arsenal when it comes to getting attention for my books. Honest feedback goes a long way in increasing visibility and helping me to reach other readers like you, so thank you in advance!

To get exclusive bonus material and be the first to hear about new releases, promotions, and giveaways **Sign up for my Newsletter at https://lmhatchell.com**

ALSO BY L.M. HATCHELL

To see the latest on all my books and upcoming publications,
visit

https://lmhatchell.com/books

www.ingramcontent.com/pod-product-compliance
Lightning Source LLC
Chambersburg PA
CBHW030757190726
48285CB00003B/898